SNIPER ELITE

ORIGINS

First published 2022 by Rebellion
an imprint of Rebellion Publishing,
Riverside House, Osney Mead, Oxford, OX2 0ES, UK
www.rebellionpublishing.com

ISBN: 978 1 78618 663 8

10 9 8 7 6 5 4 3 2 1

A CIP catalogue record for this book is available from the British
Library.

Designed & typeset by Rebellion Publishing

ISBN 978-1-78618-663-8

ORIGINS

WATER LINE

by Scott Andrews

Prologue

THE OLD SOLDIER stares at the bridge, surprised; it looms larger in his memory than in reality.

It is, at most, two truck lengths long and it is narrow, its heavy metal girders laying across old stone abutments buried deep in the banks of the canal. The stone is old, dented and pockmarked with the scars of artillery and gun fire from two different battles in two different wars.

The old soldier remembers the most recent battle all too well, and his eye traces a line of holes that run in a wavy diagonal from the waterline to the top right corner of the abutment opposite him. He remembers firing those bullets, the Bren gun punching hard into his shoulder, his ears ringing, the smell of hot metal scorching his nostrils as he fired wildly. He knows it is absurd, but he feels a slight twinge of embarrassment at the panic betrayed by that haphazard line. After that long, dark day, his marksmanship was never again so imprecise.

His destination lies over the bridge, so he steps onto it and walks slowly across. It takes less than a minute.

He turns and looks back, towards the small town of Brasee. Little remains of the settlement he remembers, and he cannot reconstruct what the enemy must have seen as they advanced towards the tiny crossing. He shakes his head, banishing old ghosts, then turns and walks on down the quiet street, which soon becomes a narrow road, then a country lane. The air is hot and full of birdsong and the buzz of insects. A left turn, and he finds a track that leads down a wooded path. After a few hundred metres the trees break to reveal an old stone farmhouse, nestled in seclusion at the edge of the woods, looking out over fields of sugar beet.

The windows are shuttered, and there are no vehicles or animals in sight.

He skirts the farmhouse, and a large wooden barn comes into view. It is padlocked.

He stands and stares at the barn, and the field that lies beyond it, for a long time.

Eventually he turns and walks away. Whatever he was looking for, he has not found it.

But then, out of the corner of his eye, he sees a flash of white and he pauses, squinting against the sunlight.

There, by a low stone wall, is a small, white gravestone.

He stares at it but does not approach.

He knows the name carved into it.

He stands there for a very long time, his eyes clouded and his breath shallow, as his memories finally, unstoppably, overwhelm him...

"'Allo? Can I help you, M'sier?'

The old soldier spins, startled out of his reverie. A woman stands in the driveway, silhouetted by sunlight. He has been so wrapped up in remembrance that he did not hear her car pull up.

'Oh, I'm sorry,' he says. 'I thought the house was empty. I was looking for Madame Defarge.'

The woman gasps and her hand flies to her mouth.

'Mon Dieu,' she mutters as she steps forward into the shadow of the house. As his eyes recover from the dazzle of sunlight and her face comes into focus, the old soldier smiles.

'Marie?' he says, incredulous.

'Monsieur Shadow?'

There is a moment of awkwardness, then she steps forward and embraces him, kissing him on both cheeks. He returns the embrace and then steps back, hands on her shoulders, shaking his head.

'I wondered...'

'Me too. I suppose we were both lucky.'

And then, simultaneously: 'What are you doing here?'

They laugh, all awkwardness gone.

'You first,' she says.

1: The Retreat

EUROPE WAS LOST, and so were we.

We had been retreating for days, harried by Messerschmitts and tanks, the Wehrmacht and the SS. By my reckoning we had passed between—and across—the constantly fluid lines multiple times as we tried to take the straightest route to Dunkirk through the chaos. Our truck was weary and full of holes and we had enough gas to take us maybe half the way to our destination. After that, we would have to walk.

There were no battle lines, no orders, and the links in the chain of command were stretching and breaking. There was just a desperate flight to the coast, the constant danger of ambush and skirmish, and whatever rearguard action could be cobbled together to delay the German onslaught and buy time for the evacuation.

At one point we came across two officers on the side of the road, a map stretched out across the bonnet of their car.

'Which way?' we asked.

'Fuck off and find your own map,' they replied before folding theirs up, jumping back in their car, and roaring away.

By this stage there were twenty-three of us rattling around, using up the last of our precious fuel, improvising a route using back roads and country lanes. I had lost count of how many men had fallen to bullets, accidents, and in one case, madness. Our rations were gone but the French farmers would stand by their fields of sugar cane with shotguns, warning us not to plunder their crops. We snuck into the fields under cover of dark and grabbed some anyway; it was that or start eating our boots.

Morale was not high.

So when our new radio operator—a beefy lad named Albert Bate, with thick black Brylcreemed hair and a Brummie twang, who had become separated from his platoon of Royal Engineers and was now tagging along with us—reported that we had been given orders to find and hold a bridge for as long as possible, many of us thought it best just to pretend we hadn't received the message and keep moving.

But Blaster wasn't going to stand for that.

Captain Frederick 'Blaster' Cast was a tall, thin man, wiry, athletic and deceptively strong. His accent was cut-glass English, the product of a public school education that emphasised proper manners and rounded vowels. He commanded with the certainty of a man who had never been tested. I wondered when the façade would begin to crack.

'What did you just say, Evans?' he said softly.

Private Evans did not back down in the face of our commanding officer's quietly measured menace.

'I said, do we have to, sir? There aren't enough of us to defend a sandcastle. We wouldn't last five minutes trying to defend a bridge.'

Blaster's face was impassive, but he didn't blink as he stared down at the young private who had just openly suggested desertion in the face of the enemy.

'I will pretend, Private Evans, that you never said that,' he said, a second after the long silence had moved from awkward to threatening.

Evans stood his ground a moment longer, then his shoulders slumped.

'Yes, sir,' he muttered. 'Thank you, sir.'

We were parked on a small, wooded lane off the road we had been travelling, and we stood around the truck stretching our legs and rubbing our sore asses. There was hardly any suspension left on the vehicle, and we had been bouncing up and down for hours on old roads and dirt tracks, crammed in the truck like cattle on the way to slaughter.

One by one we all snuck off into the cool, shaded woods to relieve our bladders against trees.

'Bate,' barked the captain, turning away from Evans, taking a map out of his breast pocket and opening it in front of him.

'Sir?'

'Where exactly is this bridge again?'

'Brasee, sir.'

Blaster peered at the map, squinting, for three long minutes before he located it.

'By my best guess,' he said eventually, 'we are about ten miles away. We can be there within the hour.'

He turned and handed the map to me.

'You can navigate, Fairburne. Give Private Evans here a rest.'

I took the map gladly; this meant I was going to be sitting up front, on a seat that at least had a little padding.

'Fucking Yank,' muttered Evans under his breath as he stalked past me.

WE HAD LEARNED to avoid the main roads because they were choked with refugees. Thousands of people, their belongings crammed into cars or loaded onto carts, clogging the highways, trying to stay ahead of the advancing German forces. But they had no more sense of where they were going than we did. Sooner or later all escape routes ended at the sea, and then what were they to do? For us, at least, there should be warships waiting to ferry us home to safety. These displaced people had no such refuge awaiting them:

they were not running to anyplace, only from.

Unfortunately, the only route to Brasee required travelling on one such road for three miles, and within seconds of nudging our way into the slow-moving human river, leaning on the horn to clear passage, we were locked into the flow and slowed to a crawl.

'And this is why I told you to stick to the back roads, Fairburne,' the captain said, leaning on the horn and attempting to wave people aside.

I did not bother to reply. I had already explained that this was the only option for this stretch of our journey and I was not in the habit of repeating myself. If he wanted to blame me for things beyond my control in order to make himself feel better, that was his prerogative as my commanding officer.

Everybody ignored the horn, then the shouting and gesturing; they just kept their heads down and shuffled onwards until Blaster drew his sidearm and fired into the air above their heads.

There was a cacophony of screaming. People scuttled and scrambled for the drainage ditches on either side of the road, gripped by blind terror. I saw one old woman trampled in the rush, her fellow travellers stamping on her heedlessly as they fled. When the road was clear of people she lay there, broken, her string bag of belongings scattered beside her on the tarmac.

The captain pretended not to see her as he pressed

on the accelerator, but I could tell he knew what he had done.

I have never been closer to shooting a senior officer than in that moment.

Blaster's callous disregard for anything but his orders didn't help speed our passage, for the road was still blocked by the vehicles and carts the cowering refugees had abandoned. All he really achieved, as he nudged the lorry forward, shoving aside the abandoned vehicles and tipping piles of crockery, clothing, candlesticks and—in one case—an upright piano into the road, was to make us into a perfect sitting duck for the Messerschmidt that dived down on us out of the sun.

The engine of the lorry drowned out the whine of the approaching plane, so it wasn't until it opened fire that we were aware of being targeted.

Bullets slammed into the road inches ahead of us, throwing up clouds of dust and hot pellets of tarmac which spattered across the windscreen, peppering the glass with tiny holes. The pilot, realising that he had pressed the fire button a second too late, pulled back quickly and began to loop around for another pass.

'Take cover!' yelled Blaster, but we were already piling out of the truck and running for the ditches. I grabbed my weapon off the seat beside me, flung myself out of the passenger door and ran to find cover behind a tree on the side of the road. I ignored the accusing looks of the refugees who crowded the ditches, cowering in unexpected silence.

I craned my neck, searching the sky for the plane, but although I could hear it now, I couldn't find it. I held my rifle tight and raised it to my shoulder. I knew that I had no realistic chance of hitting a plane in flight, but I felt as if I had to do something.

The Lee Enfield rifle that was standard issue for soldiers in the British Expeditionary Force was not a precise instrument, but it made up in stopping power what it lacked in refinement. It was heavy and sluggish and it kicked too hard when fired, but if you hit your target, the chances of them getting up again were slim. It had a simple metal pin at the end of the barrel and a flip-up sight above the trigger which you could calibrate with a little screw to help account for distance, but beyond that rudimentary assistance, it was very much a case of point, shoot and hope.

There! I could see the plane, flying low along the road, straight towards the lorry. Shooting a moving object is tricky, even with the best weapon, but it certainly helps if they are moving in a straight line at a steady speed.

I would have to shoot not at where the plane was, but at where I thought it would be when my bullet reached it. I sighted on the plane, pulled my gun to the right, aiming just ahead of it, and then kept the barrel moving, matching its flight speed. I breathed out and pulled the trigger.

I missed, of course. As I said—tricky shot, shitty weapon.

This time the pilot got his timing exactly right and his second-long volley of bullets was enough to blow our little truck sky high, along with most of the vehicles surrounding it. The blast of hot air threw me to the ground, scorching my eyebrows and showering me with debris.

The plane did a barrel roll, taunting us, and vanished into the sun to hunt for other prey.

My ears ringing, I picked myself up and walked back to the road. I stood a short distance ahead of the burning truck, waiting for my comrades to join me. By some miracle, all of them did—we had not lost anyone in the attack.

The refugees also began to emerge, dusting themselves off with weary resignation, reclaiming whatever they could from the chaos, and beginning their slow exodus once again. No one spoke to us, no one remonstrated with us for the death of the old woman, they just kept their heads down and walked hopelessly onwards.

'Right, men,' bellowed Blaster, 'we have a march of about three miles to the bridge and I want us there within the hour, so look lively!'

He turned briskly on his heel and strode ahead, not bothering to glance back to see if we were following him or not. I wish I had the unthinking confidence of the English upper class. I glanced to my left and saw Evans raising his weapon, sighting on the captain's back.

'I wouldn't do that if I were you,' I muttered.

Evans didn't look at me as he said, 'You going to stop me, are you?'

'No,' I replied. 'But how confident are you that every other soldier here would keep your secret? I may be the most unpopular man in this unit, but you're not far behind. Pull that trigger and it's a firing squad for you, take my word for it.'

'He's right, mate,' said Gunner Bate, stepping in front of Evans and staring him down.

Evans kept his gun stock in his shoulder and his eye sighting down the barrel, which was now pointing smack between Bate's eyes.

'Ah well,' he said after a long pause. 'A man can dream, can't he?' Then he lowered his gun, slung it over his shoulder and began to walk.

Bate gave me a wide-eyed grimace, let out the breath he had been holding, then winked and fell into step beside me.

And so we walked on towards our next battle.

2: The Town

'IF YOU DON'T mind me asking, why does nobody seem to like you?'

I was confused by the question. The antipathy I aroused in my fellow soldiers seemed a universal constant and I was surprised that Bate had not immediately taken a dislike to me too.

'I'm a Yank,' I said.

'So?'

'Late for the last war, late for this one,' I replied, parroting the words that had been spoken to me so often by sneering Brits.

'Well, *you're* not late, are you? How come you're here with us, then, eh?'

'Long story.'

'We've got three bloody miles, mate, and unless you want me to tell you the story of every goal I've ever scored for the Royal Engineers First Team, you might as well spill the beans.'

I laughed. It was so long since anyone had spared me a kind word. It was a relief to have someone to talk to.

'OK. My mother worked at the British Embassy in Berlin, my father at the American. In fact, he was the ambassador. Met at some embassy function, love at first sight. I came along two years later. So I have dual British and American citizenship.'

'Berlin? Blimey. Did you grow up in Germany then?'

'Until I was fifteen, yeah. By that point the writing was on the wall and my dad took us both back to the States. He didn't want me to join the Hitler Youth like a lot of my school friends were doing.'

'Oh man. So, like, any Kraut you shoot at could be one of your old school pals?'

I nodded.

'That is fucking grim, if do say so myself,' said Bate, shaking his head in wonder.

'Yeah. I try not to think about it.'

'So you can speak German?'

'Fluently.'

'You should be in intelligence then, or spook stuff, shouldn't you? What are you doing with us grunts?'

'I was at West Point…'

'Wassat?'

'Military Academy. I suppose the closest equivalent you have would be Sandhurst.'

'Bloody 'ell. Officer class, eh?' He smiled as he said it, lightly mocking.

'The US isn't the same as England, pal, trust me on that. A man like Blaster wouldn't get within spitting distance of a captain's uniform back home.'

'Oh, I dunno, rich pricks rise to the top everywhere.'

It was hard to argue with that.

'Anyway, no, I was just a soldier. It was obvious another war was coming, and I wanted to do my bit. I was just about to finish my training to join the Marines. But when war was declared, and the US refused to join, I asked my dad to pull a few strings. Because of my British citizenship he was able to get me transferred straight into the Expeditionary Force. I thought I could help.'

'But instead, everybody treats you like some Yank tourist.'

I nodded. 'Something like that.'

Bate slapped me on the arm. 'To hell with 'em,' he said. 'You turned up, that's all that matters.'

'Thanks, pal.'

We walked on in silence for a mile.

'So it was the opening game of the season,' said Bate as we crested a hill, 'and I was playing up front alongside this kid called Barker, right...'

BRASEE WAS JUST slightly too large to be a village and slightly too small to be a town. The streets were empty, but curtains twitched as we walked down Main Street.

The only people left here were those who couldn't escape, and those foolish enough to choose not to.

At the end of the street was a narrow bridge that crossed the canal, and beyond it the last few houses trailed away into woodland. The canal was wide enough to accommodate two-way traffic of the wide European barges, even if there were boats moored on either bank. It was a formidable obstacle to advancing forces and it was our job to delay them as long as possible before blowing the bridge and resuming our retreat to Dunkirk.

If we were to make our stand on this side of the water, we would have to take up firing positions in the houses on this bank, which would make us a sitting target for a tank. And while we were firing from bombarded buildings, our enemy would have much better shelter in the woods on the other side.

It was defensible, but it was going to be a bloody fight.

Blaster had taken stock of the situation, and started giving orders.

'How many Bren guns do we have?' he asked.

'Three, sir,' replied a gangly kid called, I think, Guerrier.

Blaster nodded and bit his lip. He walked out onto the bridge and turned to face the town, seeing the approach from the enemy's perspective.

'I want machine gun nests here, here and here.' He

pointed to the mouth of the bridge, a cafe to the left of it, and a house to the right. I didn't envy whoever was picked to man the gun that would be shooting directly across the bridge; they'd be the focus of all the initial fire and a tank would annihilate them with little difficulty.

'Start knocking on doors, see who's around.' He indicated a group of four soldiers standing together. 'You have permission to force entry if you think a house is unoccupied. We need sandbags or anything else that you think will help reinforce a defensive position. And tell anyone you find to clear out if they can.' He turned his attention to the rest of us.

'What ordnance do we have?' he asked.

'Lost most of it in the truck, sir,' said a squaddie called Tupper. 'This is pretty much it.'

Tupper opened his knapsack to show Blaster the contents. The captain tutted and shook his head.

'Should be enough to blow the bridge, I suppose. You and Evans, get the charges set and ready, run the fuse to that house there.' He pointed to a solid stone building on the main road—a bank, I think—sheltered from any direct fire that would be coming from the other side of the canal. 'We'll make that our HQ, for what it's worth.'

'I was hoping we'd have enough to mine the road on the other side, take care of any tanks,' muttered Bate. I grunted agreement. If a heavily armed force came down that road, the battle would be over in five minutes. Only if it was a small force would we be able to put up any meaningful resistance.

'We need a forward lookout post. I need three volunteers.'

I put my hand up. Nobody else did. I caught Bate's eye, but he grimaced and shrugged.

'Right, Fairburne, Evans and Smith,' said Blaster, selecting the two men who were most obviously attempting to make themselves invisible when he realised no one else was going to step forward. 'Head about a mile or so down the road and find a good vantage point. You radio back the second you see the enemy coming, then get back here as fast as you can. Fairburne, you see these two settled then get back here and let me know where they are.'

We nodded and set off as one, across the bridge.

THE WOODS BEGAN almost immediately we were across. As we stepped into their shade, I looked left and right, surprised and dismayed by the thickness of the trees. The defender almost always has the advantage over the attacker, but this was excellent cover. They could pick us off one by one and all we would see would be shadows and muzzle flashes.

'We should just blow the bridge now and fuck off,' said Evans as we walked.

It was hard to disagree.

We walked in silence for a couple of miles until the woods thinned and we reached a point where we could see across the mostly flat farmland for at least a couple of miles.

'This'll do,' said Smith, a short man of few words who I had never once seen smile. 'I'll climb a tree with the binoculars and keep lookout. You can wait down here with radio, alright?'

Evans grunted, failing to disguise his pleasure at avoiding any strenuous climbing.

'Be careful of the glasses,' I said to Smith. 'If they catch the sun, you'll give yourself away and they can pick you off before you even climb down.'

'When I need soldiering advice from a bloody Yank, I'll let you know, thanks,' said Smith with a sneer.

I turned and walked away.

Some people you just can't help.

ABOUT HALFWAY BACK to town I saw a woman standing at the entrance of a small track that led off the road to my right. I guessed her to be about forty, and she was clothed in a plain dress with a coat pulled tight around her shoulders.

Her arms were folded, and she stood observing me with no hint of fear as I hailed her. 'Bonjour, Mademoiselle.'

She tutted as I stopped in front of her.

'I am no mademoiselle as well you know,' she said in heavily accented English. 'And do not think I will be charmed by you, Monsieur. I am too old for such obvious flattery.'

I smiled. 'Forgive me, Madame...?'

'Defarge.'

'Forgive me, Madame Defarge, I meant no disrespect.'

She harrumphed. I thought people only did that in books, but she did it twice, so I was quite certain.

'You are American?'

I nodded. 'But I'm with the British Army.'

'Ah, I see.' Her face was a mask of disgust. 'Running away and leaving us to the Bosche.'

'Actually, we're fortifying the bridge in town, hoping to slow them down for a while.'

Her eyes widened and she scoffed. 'That is madness. They will destroy you. And what good does it do me, huh? My house, my farm and me are on this side of the bridge.' She gestured down the track, by which I gathered she lived at the end of it.

'You should leave.'

'Pah, they will go straight past me.'

'I wouldn't be so sure. They've been looting farms as they go, looking for food or... entertainment.'

She held my gaze sternly. 'They will find nothing for them at my home except bullets and cold steel.'

'Is it just you?'

She shook her head.

'You really should leave, if you can.'

'I cannot,' she replied, and for the first time I saw a hint of fear beneath the bravado. 'My father is too old to travel, and my daughter is… she is ill. Neither would survive the journey. We must take our chances.' She shrugged.

I held her gaze for a second then I reached into my holster and pulled out my sidearm, a Webley I had picked up along the way. I offered it to her, along with the few rounds of spare ammunition I had in my pack.

She was surprised by the gesture and kept her arms folded. 'You will need that, I think, Monsieur.'

Now it was my turn to shrug. 'If I am reduced to using that in the heat of battle, I'm a dead man anyway. Your need is greater. Take it. Protect yourself and your family.'

After a moment she did so, holding it awkwardly in her right hand.

'It's as simple as they come. Just point and shoot.'

She nodded. 'Thank you, Monsieur.'

'Good luck,' I said as I turned to leave.

She stepped forward and touched my arm, then embraced me as I turned back, kissing me on both cheeks.

'Bonne chance.'

I smiled, turned, and walked back towards the town.

3: The Bridge

WHEN I CROSSED the bridge back into town, I walked into the middle of a furious argument.

Blaster was standing, hands on hips, bellowing at a collection of very angry Frenchmen who had surrounded him and were gesticulating furiously as they shouted back.

I saw Bate arranging sandbags on one of the machine gun nests, and walked over to ask him what was going on.

'It's the bargemen,' he explained. 'There were loads of them hiding in their boats. So he told them to sling their hooks and go somewhere else 'cause there's gonna be a scrum, like. But they don't wanna go. Apparently, there's fighting at the bridges in both directions and nowhere safe to moor in between. They want us to blow the bridge now and get lost so the Krauts have to go somewhere else.'

I looked at the canal, with the barges filling the

waterway from bank to bank, and immediately saw the flaw in their reasoning.

I waded into the melee, pushing my way through the angry bargemen, and touched the captain on the shoulder. He spun angrily and barked, 'What?'

'Sir,' I shouted to be heard above the din, 'even if we blow the bridge, the Germans can cross using the barges. They'd have to leave their vehicles, but foot soldiers can hop across using the boats. And they can quickly outflank us from either direction.'

He looked at the canal and realised I was right. The barges were so tightly packed that they formed a long bridge in and of themselves. I assumed that upon realising this, he'd just blow the bridge and leave. But there was an option I had not considered.

Pulling his sidearm from his holster, the captain fired a shot in the air. The bargemen fell silent.

'You have five minutes to get your barges moving, or we will destroy them,' he shouted at the red-faced Frenchmen.

Predictably, this just provoked more shouting. After a few more minutes of this, Blaster pushed his way out of the throng, pointed at Guerrier, Bate and me, and barked, 'Right, burn the lot!'

'Sir, won't that attract attention, like? Let the Germans know we're here?' said Bate.

'Is everyone going to question my orders today?' shouted Blaster, his voice breaking into an awful squeak as his pitch rose. 'Burn the bloody lot of them, and if anybody tries to stop you, shoot them!'

Bate and Guerrier hurried away towards the barges and I followed, pursued by the angry bargemen. Most of the boats had red petrol cans on the stern next to the engines. All we would have to do was spread that about a bit and then light a match. The whole canal would go up.

I thought about suggesting that we wait and light them only when we knew the Germans were approaching, so we could use the smoke as cover, but Blaster wasn't in a listening mood and I figured it was best just to follow orders.

I wasn't going to shoot any civilians though.

'Let's stick together,' I said to Bate as some bargemen got in front of us and tried to bar the way.

A standoff quickly developed, with the bargees standing at the water's edge, linking arms defiantly while Bates, Guerrier and I stood facing them, our rifles in our hands. A tense silence fell until one of the bargees stepped forward and spat in Guerrier's face.

'Right, sod this,' said Guerrier as he pulled back the bolt on his Lee-Enfield before slamming it into place, chambering a round.

'You can't,' protested Bate.

'Can't what?' replied Guerrier. 'Can't follow orders? Be a bloody soldier, man. If these boats stay here the enemy will use them to cross. By stopping us destroying them, these Frenchies are offering aid to the enemy and that makes them traitors as far as I'm concerned. To hell with them.'

He raised his rifle to his shoulder but Bate leaned across and grabbed the barrel, pulling it down.

'You can't!' spat Bate.

Guerrier pulled back on the rifle, dragging Bate towards him, then jabbed it forward. It hit hard in Bate's shoulder and he stumbled backwards, falling to ground.

Guerrier raised his gun again, this time aiming at Bate.

I tightened my grip on my weapon, ready to move.

'You're as much a traitor as they are,' yelled Guerrier. 'Do you want to die here? The whole bloody German army is coming this way and if we don't...'

And then the back of his head exploded.

We heard the report of the shot a split second later, while the cloud of blood and brains was still ballooning outwards. Then there was an awful silence as we all stood transfixed, and Guerrier crumpled to the ground with a wet smack.

'Sniper!' I yelled, and everyone scattered.

I ran for the nearest house as more shots rang out, putting my shoulder down and charging at the front door. It shattered and gave as I hit it and I tumbled inside, scrambling out of the light into the shadows of the living room.

I took a moment to catch my breath, then crawled to the window. There were lace curtains and the sun was shining on the canal from behind the house, so I figured there was little chance the sniper would be able to see me.

The canal-side path was deserted. I reckoned the bargemen must have run into town, as I could see no one cowering on the barges. I scanned for more corpses and there was one other dead soldier, besides Guerrier. I was relieved when I saw that it wasn't Bate, and I hoped he'd made it to safety.

I waited and watched. I had no idea where the sniper was hiding, so my eyes roved along the trees. We had received no radio warning from Evans and Smith, so this sniper had either snuck past them or killed them. Either way, the rest of the German forces could not be far behind.

I caught an impression of movement from the bridge and when I squinted, I could see two of my comrades hiding underneath it; they had been trapped while laying the charges. There was no way for them to safely re-enter the town, which meant the sniper only had to keep us all pinned down until the first reinforcements arrived, and the bridge would be taken.

There was no time to wait. Something had to be done fast.

Another shot, and I caught the flash of the muzzle,

deep and high in the trees off to my right, on the other side of the bridge. If I made a run for it, I could perhaps make it across the barges and come at him through the trees, but it was a slim chance. Most likely he'd pick me off the moment I broke cover. I needed a distraction.

The barges were my only way across, but how to make it safely?

I crawled away from the window, then began to search the house. It did not take me long to find a bottle of Calvados, and within a minute I had an improvised Molotov cocktail. I edged my way forward to the very edge of the shadow of the doorway and sighted my rifle at the barges. I could see four petrol cans available to me. A moving plane may have been too much of a challenge, but a few petrol cans gently bobbing up and down on a calm canal were well within the capabilities of even my old Lee Enfield .303. I methodically shot each one in turn. The first two only began to leak, but the third and fourth exploded with a soft, satisfying crump. Then I stood back, heaved my Molotov at the boat nearest me, and enjoyed the soft whoosh of flames as it lit that boat on fire. It soon caught the fuel spilled by my first two bullets, and within a minute the canal was a wall of fire and thick, billowing smoke that completely hid me from the sniper's gaze.

Or at least, that was the theory.

I took a deep breath, aimed myself at the barges just beyond the nearest edge of the fire, and ran for all I was worth.

Across the pathway to the first flame-free barge. I leapt onto the roof and scrambled across, keeping low just in case. It was a simple hop to the next barge and then again to the final one. There was a small footpath on the bank ahead of me, then the trees began. The smoke was still hiding me as I crouched on the barge, preparing to make a break for the woods. The wind was blowing the smoke towards the town, so the second I hit the path, I would be exposed. But it was unlikely the sniper would be able to see me. Unlikely, but not impossible.

I took a deep breath and jumped for the bank. I was in the trees within seconds, and no bullets came whistling past me.

Now for the tricky part. I would have to make my way through the woods towards the sniper without making a sound and staying in cover at all times. It was possible he had a spotter with him, or somebody on the ground to defend his position against someone like me. If I hurried or was careless, I'd be dead before I even heard the shot that killed me.

I moved slowly and carefully. The fire on the barges was out of control now and the roar of the blaze—and the explosions as engines and petrol cans succumbed—provided some aural cover but I still made sure I didn't step on any snappable twigs. The light of the inferno cast wild, dancing shadows in the trees, which would make it harder for the sniper to see me as I advanced towards his position.

I knew roughly where my target was placed, but only roughly. The closer I got, the more danger I would be in.

A shot rang out from somewhere ahead of me, but the noise and smoke and shadows that gave me cover also helped him; it was hard to pinpoint where the shot had come from. I crept forward, crouched down, rifle ready, moving cautiously from one tree to the next, scanning both the ground ahead of me, and the canopy above until I reached the road.

I glanced right. So far, the fire had not reached the bridge, so the two soldiers cowering beneath it could not yet have made it to safety. Smoke drifted across the road, though, so I figured they would be able to make a run for it soon. I could see across the bridge into town, and there was no movement at all. Everyone was hiding from the sniper. I looked left, fearing that I might see a tank or a cadre of SS advancing down the road towards the bridge, but it was empty. I still had time.

I had seen the muzzle flash of the sniper's shot about ten meters beyond the road. Assuming he had not moved, I was now definitely within hearing distance and there was a chance he might register movement out of the corner of his eye as I crossed the road. But time was of the essence, so I took a deep breath and sprinted across. Immediately a bullet hit the ground at my feet, throwing up a cloud of dirt. Stupid - I hadn't considered that my unit might see me and assume I was the sniper. I dived for the trees and rolled into the undergrowth as more bullets pinged around me.

I leant against a tree and took deep breaths, calming myself. That would have alerted my target, he would now be on his guard. Dammit.

I risked a glance around the tree I was hiding behind, but all I could see were shadows. Did he know where I was? Was he just waiting for me to break cover? I sat there for a long minute, but I knew deep down that it made no difference how long I hesitated: the risk would be the same.

I looked again and saw no movement, so I took a deep breath and crept out from behind the tree.

Instantly, a bullet thudded off the trunk of the tree just beside my face, peppering my cheek with splinters. Without thinking I rolled away, brought my rifle up and fired a single shot towards the place in the trees where I had seen the glint of the muzzle.

There was a grunt and then the sound of branches snapping as my opponent tumbled to earth.

I sighed with relief but continued moving to cover in case he was not alone. But there was no sound to indicate the presence of another German. Yet as

I listened intently for anything that might betray the presence of a spotter, I heard something else. Echoing down the road came the soft, distant, but unmistakable rumble of a tank.

The main force had arrived.

4: The Tank

I RAN TO the place where the sniper had fallen. I could see that I had shot him in the leg, so I couldn't claim the kill—it was the fall that had killed him. He had been pretty smashed by the branches on his descent, so I didn't linger on details, just rifled desperately through his pack for anything useful. By sheer, brilliant chance there was a single landmine in there. It wasn't much, but it was better than nothing.

I ran back to the road and crawled out onto it, placing the mine as close to the head of the bridge as I could, roughly where I hoped the tank's caterpillar track would trigger it. I scooped some dirt on top of it, before edging back into the woods and sprinting some distance along the canal, then hopped and scrambled over the barges, and ran back towards the gun nests, waving and shouting so that nobody could mistake me for the enemy.

'I've taken care of the sniper but there's a tank coming.

Battle positions!' I yelled.

I didn't wait to see the response, instead shooting all the petrol cans I could see, spreading the blaze and making sure that it burnt hard on either side of the bridge. No bargemen ran to stop me; I assumed they were all running for their lives by now.

I reached the bridge again, sheltering behind the stonework, and shouted to the two men who had been pinned down while planting the charges.

'Charges set?'

One guy poked his head out and shook it. 'Another ten minutes at least.'

'Then leave it, you're out of time. Get back up here.'

He didn't need telling twice, and he and his colleague scrabbled out and up onto the road.

By this time Blaster had broken cover and was rallying the men behind me, assigning them to the various machine gun nests. I hurried to the one on the right-hand side of the bridge and took up position behind the Bren gun. A moment later Bate and another soldier—a tall, spotty kid called Fred—joined me.

'One tank at least, I don't know how many men and support vehicles,' I said, without waiting for them to ask what was coming.

'A tank? We're buggered then,' said Bate. 'We've got no chance.'

'Maybe one,' I said. 'I mined the road.'

Bate beamed. 'Nice work.'

We waited as the rumble grew louder, knowing that our guns would have no effect on the armour plating of the mechanical giant bearing down on us.

'Concentrate your fire on the track on your right!' yelled Blaster. 'We need to break the tank's caterpillars, get it stuck if we can.'

We all knew what a vain hope that was, but I sighted my gun and waited to open fire the moment the tank came into view. The rumble grew louder, like approaching thunder, and I am not ashamed to admit that I felt butterflies in my stomach. I had trained long and hard to prepare myself for combat, but so far all I had experienced in this shambolic war were long distance skirmishes; someone taking potshots at me as I did the same in return. Now it finally seemed like I was about to find myself in the thick of close-quarter fighting. Would I be up to the task? Would I fail and run? Fall victim to a stray bullet fired from who-knew-where? Would I look into the eyes of a stranger as he buried a knife in my heart?

I tightened my grip on the Bren gun, ready for the pounding in my shoulder, the deafening clatter in my ears, the overwhelming smell of cordite and hot metal. Ready to find out if I really had what it took to fight a war.

The tank rumbled into view, its mighty gun emerging from the shadows of the trees, ploughing relentlessly towards the bridge. Then it stopped, just before it moved onto the old stone crossing.

I cursed. It hadn't hit my mine.

I could see no movement behind it. Had it come on ahead of the men, or were they hanging back on the road or in the woods, waiting for the tank to clear a path?

'Fire!' yelled Blaster, and I tugged back on the trigger.

The noise was deafening as all three Bren guns opened fire at once, pouring fire on the nearest visible spot of tread to our right. One man in the machine gun nest at the bridge's mouth stood and tossed a grenade at the tank, but it shrugged off the explosion, lowered its gun and with a single massive boom sent that man and his fellows straight to hell.

'Shoot at the gunner's window,' I yelled to Bate, indicating the small slot through which the gunner was choosing his targets. Disobeying orders, I swung my Bren gun up and to the left and used the tracer bullets to inch my way closer to the slot, hoping to take out the gunner before he could do too much more damage.

The gun turret began to rotate towards our position, but the trees prevented it getting a bead on us, so it inched forward slowly, creeping onto the bridge and shimmying slightly to the left to allow the gun a wider angle of fire. And praise be, this manoeuvre brought its tracks over the mine I had laid. There was a soft crump, and a cloud of smoke and debris rose from the rear of the tank.

I knew it was unlikely that this had killed everyone inside, but the tank was stuck fast, blocking the bridge, and for a few precious moments its occupants would be stunned by the sound of the blast as it bounced around inside their tin can. Seeing an opportunity, I leapt up, jumped over the sandbags and sprinted as fast as I could across the bridge, pulling a grenade from my belt and pinging out the pin as I ran.

The tank's machine gun could have cut me in half, but I was gambling that everyone inside was still reeling from the mine's blast. I vaulted up onto the tank and shoved the grenade through the gunner's little slot window, then flung myself backwards off the tank, hitting the ground in front of it as the grenade exploded, shredding everyone inside.

I lay there for a moment, half deafened and breathing hard. The gunfire had stopped, and there was a moment of surreal calm. Once I had caught my breath I clambered to my feet and peered around the tank to look down the road. There was no sign of soldiers or more tanks, but they couldn't be far behind.

I turned and walked back across the bridge to my unit, who were emerging from all their places of concealment. Blaster walked up to me and nodded his head in reluctant acknowledgment.

'Good work, Fairburne,' he said grudgingly, pushing his hat back on his head.

I didn't trust myself to speak. My whole body was vibrating with adrenalin and I could feel my hands shaking slightly. So I nodded and went to sit down by Bate to take a moment.

'You all right, mate?' asked Bate as I slumped to the ground.

'Ask me in ten minutes,' I gasped. He slapped me on the shoulder as I closed my eyes.

I had answered my own question simply and without ambiguity. I was definitely capable of fighting this war. But I didn't feel pride so much as a presentiment of bone-deep weariness as I realised what the years ahead would hold were I lucky enough to stay alive. Because I knew that now I had proven myself to myself, I would throw myself headfirst into combat at every opportunity.

Mine was definitely not going to be a short or a safe war. I needed to take a moment to register that and make peace with it, because I knew that was the only peace I was likely to feel for a long, long time.

And, as if on cue, the guns began firing again.

5: The Battle

MACHINE GUN FIRE streamed across the bridge from behind the still-smoking tank. But with the barges aflame and the bridge blocked, there was no way for the forces on the other side of the canal to fire with any accuracy. We all took cover, but for now our position seemed pretty much unassailable.

But while the smoke and flames provided us with cover, they also prevented us from assessing the size of the opposing force. We had no idea how many men were massing across the water, how well equipped they were, or what kind of threat they posed.

'We need to burn more barges,' said Bate. 'Before they can use them to outflank us.'

He was right. The barges were ablaze for about fifty meters or so on either side of the bridge, but they stretched away for some distance beyond that in each direction, and though the fire was spreading, it would be easy for the Germans to get beyond the fire, hop across the boats and outflank us.

Without waiting for orders, Bate and I crouched down and headed for the edge of the blaze to our left, leaving Fred to man the Bren gun.

The wind had shifted and the smoke from the burning boats was blowing towards us now, which made our throats burn and our eyes stream, but we pushed through until we reached the edge of the conflagration. The instant we emerged from the smoke, bullets began pinging all around us and we ran into the nearest house and took cover.

Sure enough the Germans were ahead of us, firing at us from the treeline on the opposite bank. There was no sign of a force making the crossing yet, but if these soldiers could keep us pinned down long enough for their men to muster, and prevent us from torching the remaining barges, we would be in deep trouble.

It was a simple living room. Open fireplace, two armchairs, a table and a rug. A few framed pictures stood on the mantelpiece commemorating the wedding of the couple who had lived here and who were now no doubt part of the refugee tide. And now it was covered in glass, and there were holes in the walls and plaster raining down on everything. And soon it would burn to the ground.

'I'll shoot the petrol cans from upstairs,' I shouted, as the glass in the windows shattered above our heads. 'You find any alcohol you can and make some Molotovs.'

Bate gave me a thumbs up, and we both crawled away from the window, deeper into the house. The staircase was narrow and uncarpeted, and I pounded up the stairs and into a bedroom where a small double bed sat under a floral counterpane. I crawled underneath the window and stood to one side, back against the wall and craned my head around to look down at the canal.

The smoke made it hard to see clearly, but there were barges crammed into the canal three abreast for at least another hundred meters. I caught glimpses of petrol cans through the murk. I raised my rifle and smashed the window, then knelt and took aim, careful to stay out of the line of enemy fire. I had to time each shot to coincide with a break in the smoke, so it was time-consuming and tricky. And, as before, not all the petrol canisters exploded, some just toppled over and began to leak.

It did not take the enemy long to work out where I was firing from, and a stream of bullets came screaming through the window, disintegrating the frame and turning the far wall into powder. But I kept firing, confident their bullets couldn't touch me as long as I kept my position.

I succeeded in setting four more barges alight, but it wasn't nearly enough. Then there was a clatter to my left and I turned to see a grenade rolling under the bed. I had no choice but to vault out the window, plummeting to the street as the room exploded above my head and bullets sang around me. I scrambled back through the front door, chunks of ceiling raining down on me from the burning bedroom above, and I hurried to the back of the house.

Bate was in the kitchen, filling the last of a row of eight empty beer bottles from a paraffin can.

'Getting a bit hairy out there, innit?' he said cheerfully.

I coughed up a bolus of plaster and dirt and nodded weakly.

'Rip that up then,' he said, indicating a towel that lay draped across the simple cooking range.

I tore the towel into strips, and we stuffed them into the necks of the bottles.

'Right,' said Bate, when all our Molotovs were ready. 'I reckon we nip out the back and we go house to house, chucking these out the front doors as we go till we get to the end of the boats.'

'Sounds like a plan,' I said, gathering up four of the bottles and leading the way out the back door into a small but well-kept garden, bordered by a low stone wall. A gate in the rear wall led into a lane, and it was easy to then pop through the gate into next door's garden, and then in through their back door. I carefully unlatched the front door of this house— better furnished than its neighbour, with carpet and more ornate picture frames—lit the rag on the first bomb, then cracked the door open, lobbed the bomb onto the nearest barge not yet aflame, then slammed the door shut and fled to the rear of the house as the front door was turned to matchwood by enemy fire.

Bate was emerging from next door as I did, and we leapfrogged each other like this, house to house to the end of the row. Now we had a problem. We each had one bomb left, but we had reached a road that led to the canal side. On the other side of the road was a single house, larger than most we had seen, and it clearly marked the edge of the town. Somehow, we had to get to a point where we could throw our bombs safely to hit the last few barges, but neither of us could see a way to do it without exposing ourselves to enemy fire.

I peered around the edge, ready to run for it, only to see a cadre of German SS troops clambering across the barges towards us. I stepped back quickly.

'SS on the boats,' I said to Bate. His eyes widened, then he held up his beer bottle and smiled. I ignited my trusty Zippo, lit the rags on our Molotovs, then on the count of three we jumped out into the road and heaved our bombs at them.

Bate's aim was terrible and his bomb soared over the canal and blossomed into flame on the opposite bank.

'Sorry,' he said. 'More used to kicking things than throwing them.'

My aim was true, however, and my Molotov

exploded in the midst of the advancing soldiers. The screams were truly terrible. A few of them ran for the end of the barges, flinging themselves into the canal water and sinking without a trace. The rest thrashed and flailed and screamed and died.

I risked running to the canal side, keeping myself close to the wall of the farthest house, and checking the barges. All were blazing fiercely, and a wall of flame separated one bank of the canal from the other, all the way from the bridge to the end of the moored boats.

I hurried back to Bate.

'Done,' I said. 'No Germans are getting across the canal this side of the bridge.'

'We should get back,' said Bate, gesturing towards the bridgehead, from which we could hear sustained gunfire.

Too tired to run, we allowed ourselves the luxury of walking back.

'D'you reckon someone thought to do the same thing on the other side of the bridge?' asked Bate.

'I hope so,' I replied. 'Because if not...'

There was no need to finish the sentence because we rounded the last house onto the main road and found ourselves the sudden focus of an awful lot of gunfire.

'SHIT!' Bate grabbed my arm and pulled me back into a doorway.

At the doorways and windows of all the buildings on the other side of the main street were SS troops, raining fire across the road. Bullets pinged off the stone as Bate and I crammed ourselves into the tiny alcove. I tried the door handle, but it was locked tight. I lifted my rifle, chambered a round, then pointed it down at the lock at an awkward angle, anxious not to expose even an elbow to the enemy gunmen. I fired, the lock shattered, and Bate and I tumbled inside, landing in a tangled heap.

A soldier who had been crouched at the window returning enemy fire was startled by our entrance and spun, firing wildly at us. He was too panicked to be accurate, and before I had chance to wave at him and shout that we were friendlies a hail of bullets tore into him through the window and he jerked and fell to the floor, twitching as he bled out.

'What the fuck is going on?' yelled Bate, beginning to show the first signs of panic I'd seen from him as we untangled ourselves and scrambled to the wall.

'They must have come across the barges further down the canal before the others had chance to torch them,' I said.

'I bet that idiot Blaster never even gave the bleeding order.'

He was probably right. I cursed myself for not taking a moment to shout our intentions to the others before leaving the machine gun nest. But then again, we had cut it so fine that even those few seconds could have allowed the SS to cross on our side of the bridge too, which would have made the situation even worse. As if it could be much worse!

'We need to get out of here,' I said. 'There's no way we can hold the town. We've got to retreat. The bridge is lost.'

Bate nodded.

'Do we try to regroup, or is it every man for himself, do you reckon?'

As I was about to answer the gunfire suddenly stopped. An eerie silence fell and then we heard a voice shouting in German-accented English.

'You are outnumbered, outgunned and outflanked,' came the echoing voice. 'You do nobody any good by dying here. And you will die. I will allow your commanding officer to surrender on your behalf. You have my word that you will be treated properly in accordance with the rules of war.'

'Und if you believe zat,' muttered Bate in a mock German accent, 'I can sell you Poland for only two million marks!'

He was right. Had this been the ordinary German Army we were fighting, the Wehrmacht, then maybe we could have trusted them to behave as gentlemen. But anybody who expected anything but ruthless expediency from the SS was a damned fool.

So it was little surprise to me when I heard Blaster's voice booming out into the street.

'We surrender!'

6: The Surrender

IT'S ONE THING to surrender, it's quite another to organise it.

Do you all lay down arms and walk out empty-handed while the enemy still have their guns trained on you? Or does your commanding officer walk out and meet the enemy's commanding officer in no-man's-land, where they shake hands and negotiate the terms? Either way, there's nothing to stop them gunning you down as soon as you're all present and correct.

Bate and I exchanged glances, then simultaneously shook our heads. We weren't going to be anybody's shooting practice.

'Do we run for it?' he asked.

I considered our options. Whichever way we exited the house—out the front door onto Main Street, or via the side doors onto either the canal path or the side street—we would most likely be seen by the SS. On the other hand, they were sure to do a house to house search, and there was little chance of us concealing ourselves successfully.

I nodded reluctantly. 'Yeah, I think so.'

'Canal path's the best bet,' said Bate. 'Smoke should give us some cover.'

It was a slim chance, but he was right: it was the only logical choice.

'OK. We wait and pick our moment,' I said.

We crawled through the house to the canal-side door and checked that it was unlocked, then I took up position at the window, careful not to give away our location, so I could see the main street. A moment later Blaster appeared, walking out into the middle of the road with his hands up.

'We surrender ourselves and expect to be treated in accordance with the Geneva Convention,' he said loudly.

For a moment all was quiet and still as everyone waited to see what would happen next. Then the doors of the houses on the opposite side of the street began to open and SS troopers emerged from the buildings, machine guns raised and ready to fire.

A tall, thin man in an SS officer's uniform stepped forward from the pack and offered his hand for Blaster to shake, which he did. They talked for a moment, voices low so I couldn't hear.

'Now's our chance,' I whispered. 'While everyone's watching them.'

Bate didn't need telling twice and cracked the door open quietly. We shuffled out onto the canal path and began to make our way along it, crouching low and keeping close to the buildings, careful not to make any noise. Some of the barges had begun to sink, but most were still burning fiercely and the biggest risk of revealing ourselves was the coughing fits we had to keep choking back as the smoke drifted across our path. No alarm was shouted, and we made it safely to the large house at the end of the road where we had burned the SS soldiers a few minutes before. We ducked off the path and gratefully straightened up, safely out of earshot of the soldiers on the main street.

'So what do we do now?' asked Bate. 'Keep heading for the coast?'

I considered it. It was likely there would be little we could do to help the rest of the unit, and we did no good by getting ourselves captured. But I didn't feel good about running away. No matter how wise it was, no matter how much my unit disliked me, it felt wrong to abandon them to the tender ministrations of the SS.

'I think I'm going to stick around, keep an eye on them,' I said. 'But you should go. See if you can find another unit who might be able to come and help, perhaps.'

'Fat chance,' replied Bate. 'Nah, if you'm staying, then so am I. What's the plan, though?'

'Stay out of sight, find out where they're holding everyone, see if we can free them somehow. I worry about what the SS might do. From their perspective it might be quicker and easier to just kill them and move on.'

'They wouldn't do that, would they?'

I shrugged, non-committal.

'So how do we keep an eye on them without being spotted? I don't have any binoculars. Do you?' he asked.

'I have an idea about that,' I said. 'I killed the sniper who was pinning us down earlier. If I can get to the body and get hold of his rifle, the scope would allow us to keep our distance. And maybe even the score if they start getting trigger happy.'

'So where's the sniper's body?'

'Other side of the canal, other side of the bridge.'

Bate stared at the burning barges. 'And we're going to get there how, exactly?'

THE WATER WAS cold and muddy. I tried to lower myself in without ducking my head underwater, because the last thing I wanted was a mouth full of canal. It was not a particularly wide waterway, and because it was a canal rather than a river there was no current to contend with. I just tried to think of it as a deep, cloudy lido as I swam across it breaststroke. We had scavenged bags from a cottage we had passed as we moved away from the town, and I was holding mine, with my clothing and kit in it, as much above the water as I could.

Climbing out on the opposite bank was harder than I'd expected, and my hands slipped back on the mud and grass many times before I finally got purchase and was able to haul myself onto dry land. I stood and waved at Bate, who grinned and jumped in enthusiastically, submerging himself entirely with a loud splash and surfacing with a stupid grin on his face before he, too, swam across. He handed me his bag and I hauled him ashore.

We had travelled about a mile beyond the town to be sure that we could cross without risk of being spotted, but it meant we now had to make our way back to the road, and across it safely, if we were to locate the sniper and his rifle. Assuming, that is, he hadn't been located and looted by the SS as they had advanced on the town.

Bate and I dressed, shivering, and began the slow, careful journey back towards the bridge through the woods staying just within the treeline, close to the canal. It was quiet and still and there was none of the birdsong you would normally expect in such a setting; the shooting and the fires must have scared them all off. It was eerie and unsettling, as if we were walking towards a place that even nature had abandoned.

When we reached the farthest of the burning barges, we knew we were close. The boats had almost all sunk, but the canal was not deep, and the wreckage of the barges had piled up on itself, planks and beams poking up out of the water like charred bones. The smell of petrol and burnt tar was nauseating.

Now that we were close, we moved deeper into the woods and slowed our pace even more, watching the forest floor before we took each step, careful not to give ourselves away with a twig snap, while also scanning ahead and above for sentries or lookouts. We moved methodically, silently, towards the road we would have to cross.

As we approached the road, I heard noises coming from up ahead. I indicated for Bate to stop and wait, and I crawled forward on my belly, careful to stay within the shadows, until I could see what was happening.

Two German trucks were trying to tow the wreckage of the tank off the bridge to clear the way for them to progress across it, but their efforts were not going smoothly. The jagged metal wheels, damaged by the mine, were digging deeper into the hard ground as the trucks pulled, making it impossible to move. My pleasure at the damage and delay my efforts had caused was tempered by the fact that the two trucks both had German soldiers with them—two driving, the other two watching the ropes and directing their efforts.

I crawled back to Bate.

'Four Germans,' I told him.

'We could go down the road a bit and cross where they can't see us,' he suggested.

I shook my head. 'There must be more soldiers on the way, and chances are we'd just run into them. And even if we didn't, I don't want to risk losing the time. We'll have to kill them.'

Bate blanched at this. 'Won't that give us away, though?'

'If we move quickly and quietly,' I replied, drawing my knife, 'we can be gone before anyone realises.'

Bate hesitated and I could sense his reluctance, but he eventually drew his own blade and nodded. Together we crawled back to the road. Two men were inspecting the ropes and debating next steps while the two drivers were sitting in the truck cabs, smoking.

'We take those two first,' I said, indicating the men by the ropes. 'Then we take the guys in the trucks.'

Bate nodded and I led the way, crawling through the woods along the road till we lay parallel to the two men, both of whom had their backs to us, as luck would have it. Gesturing for Bate to stay put, I leant out and scanned the road in each direction. The tank still blocked the bridge and there was enough smoke still rising from the smouldering debris of the barges to ensure that we could not be seen from the town.

It was now or never.

I had gone through these motions countless times. The slow approach, keeping low, the spring upright, the hand across the mouth as the knife slides silently up between the target's ribcage into the heart. I had done it over and over so often that it was burned into my muscle memory. But it had always been a wooden knife and a willing target playing along for training purposes. I had never gotten blood on my hands, felt a dying man's breath escape between my fingers, borne the weight of him as he collapsed into me and the life left his body. I clenched my teeth, steadied my nerves and, with a curt nod to Bate, broke cover, stalking my prey with cold steel in my hand.

I wondered if it helped that Bate didn't understand German. As he approached his target, all he heard was gibberish, making it easier not to humanise the man he was about to kill, whereas I could understand every word. The man on the right, my target, was telling the guy on his left about his wife, Inga, who had just given birth to their first child, a daughter they had named Hannelore. He was removing a photo from his breast pocket when I rose up behind him, smothered his mouth and sliced through his left ventricle.

He gasped and struggled, but he quickly went limp, his head lolling backwards and his shoulders following. I was not prepared for the weight of him to move in such a way and I had not braced my legs correctly. He overbalanced me and we toppled in a heap on the road, his twitching corpse briefly pinning me to the ground.

I threw him off, alarmed that the men in the trucks might look in their wing mirror and spy me wriggling around, murdering their friend. The body of my victim slid off me and I rose to a crouch and grabbed his legs, dragging him behind the trucks and out of sight. As I did so, Bate was doing the same. I could see he had managed better than I, having avoided falling over and making a spectacle of himself as I had done.

We laid the bodies down and exchanged a glance. Bate was as white as a sheet and I daresay I was too. It's one thing to kill a man with a bullet from long distance; quite another to do it up close and personal, where you can feel the warmth of their body as you extinguish their life. It was something I would have to get used to though, not least because now I had to do it again straight away.

I pointed for Bate to cross the ropes and take the driver in the far truck. He nodded and stepped over the ropes, wiping his knife on his sleeve as he did so. I turned and sidled around the edge of the truck, pressing myself flat against it as I sidestepped towards the cab. This was going to be tricky. I would have to open the door and pull him from the cab down onto the road and stab him once he was down. If I fumbled this, he could pull away from me and draw a weapon, or perhaps lean on the horn and alert the soldiers in town; in either instance Bate and I would be as good as dead.

I stood beside the door, breathing in the smoke he was puffing out the cab window, preparing myself. But as I looked down, I saw a chunk of metal—a piece of caterpillar track blown off the tank - and an idea occurred to me. I bent down and picked it up, then threw it as hard as I could at the nearest tree. It made a loud clatter as it struck and then fell to the floor. I waited, holding my breath, waiting to see if my target would take the bait.

Sure enough I heard him mutter, 'Was war das?' Then the door handle popped, and he began to climb out of the cab backwards, placing his foot on the small metal footboard. I stepped out and forward, grabbed him by the back of his shirt and pulled him backwards. He crashed to the road, winded and stunned, and I had my knife in his heart before he could utter a sound. His eyes stared up at me, wide in shock and horror as he gurgled and spasmed.

When he fell silent, still staring into my eyes, I heard sounds of a struggle behind me. I jumped up and ran around the truck to find Bate on the ground, pinned down by the truck driver, who had somehow turned the knife on him. Bate was struggling to hold back the knife as the German put all his weight on it, forcing it down towards his chest. Before I could reach them, the German reared back and then flung himself down, overwhelming Bate's strength. Luckily Bate took advantage of the momentary release of pressure to try and roll away so the knife did not penetrate his heart, but it struck hard into his left shoulder, sliding across his collar bone as I heard a nasty crack.

The German pulled the knife back out and was ready to deliver the killing blow, but he was not aware of me coming up behind him, and my knife was in his neck, pulling him backwards and off Bate even as he began his downward thrust. My knife caught on the man's spine as I pulled backwards, and lodged in between the bones as he bled out without ever seeing the face of his killer.

I wrenched my knife out—which was harder than I thought it would be—and went to see to Bate. He was lying there with blood gushing out of a deep, long wound that ran along the line of his collarbone and down into his arm.

'Shit shit shit shit shit shit,' he was saying through clenched teeth.

I reached into my pack and pulled out a roll of bandage. It wasn't much, but I needed to get the wound bound as quickly as possible while I worked out what to do with him.

'Sit up,' I said urgently, but he lay there grimacing, his eyes starting to glaze over. I slapped him hard to jolt him back to consciousness. 'I said sit up and don't you dare pass out on me!'

He grunted and did his best to rise but was unable. I grabbed the front of his jacket and poured him up to a sitting position, then began wrapping the bandage as tightly as I could around his injury. When I was done I asked him, 'Do you think you can walk?'

He nodded. His face was ghostly white, his breath came in short, jagged gasps, and his eyes stared at me with a mix of desperation and determination.

'OK, we need to get away from here before someone raises the alarm, then we need to get you patched up before you lose too much blood. So come on.'

I stood and bent down to pull him up, my arms under his shoulders. He grunted with pain again as I dragged him to his feet. Throwing his right arm around my shoulder, and with my left arm around his waist, I walked him as fast as I could back into the trees.

'Where we going?' he stuttered as I half-carried him along.

'I think I know somewhere we can rest up,' I said as I kept us moving deeper into the woods.

The going was slow and hard. It felt like Bate was becoming heavier and weaker with every step he took, but I took up the strain, determined that he would not die on me. Shortly we came to a narrow mud track, and I turned us left. If I had got my bearings right, this was the track that led to the house where Madame Defarge was sheltering with her father and daughter.

It was the only place I could think of to go, and I hoped beyond hope that we would find sanctuary there.

7: The Sanctuary

THE FARMHOUSE WAS made of stone and seemed almost
to be part of the landscape, waiting at the edge of the
woods, skirted by trees, surveying the fields beyond
with ancient, paternal care.

There were blue wooden shutters on all the
windows, and they had been closed. No smoke rose
from the chimney, no vehicles were parked outside.
Unless I had known it to be occupied, I would have
assumed it empty. Madame Defarge was doing
everything she could not to attract attention. I hoped,
for her sake and for mine, that it worked.

Bate was a dead weight now, barely conscious,
and it was all I could do to keep him upright and
moving, but progress was slow. I did not want to risk
shouting for help, so I dragged him to the nearest
door and knocked on it. There was no response,
and no sound of movement from inside. I pictured
the inhabitants, frozen in fear; one of them perhaps

holding a shotgun, Madame Defarge with my Webley in her hand.

'Madame Defarge,' I said to the impassive door. 'It's me, the soldier you met earlier. I need your help, please. I have a man in need of urgent medical assistance. I know you can hear me, please let us in. If you don't, he's a dead man.'

There was a long pause, and I almost gave up, but then I heard the sound of bolts being drawn back and the door swung open to reveal Madame Defarge, gun in hand.

'Quickly,' she said, ushering us in.

I dragged Bate over the threshold into the shaded cool of a large kitchen. A tall, thin elderly man stood by a large wooden kitchen table, slightly stooped and propped up by a walking cane. A young girl, no more than ten, was busy clearing the table of crockery and condiments. The man gestured to Bate, who had collapsed on the floor, and then to the table. I understood his meaning and once the table was clear I lifted my friend on to it and stood upright, my back and shoulders burning from the strain of carrying him all this distance.

The old man produced a pair of tailor's scissors and waved them at Madame Defarge, who by now had closed the door. He spoke urgently to her in French as she took the scissors. She replied and began to cut the jacket and shirt off Bate.

'My father does not speak English, but he is a doctor,' she explained as she cut the blood-soaked fabric away. 'Was a doctor, I should say. He was in the trenches.'

She did not say any more, but she did not need to. By sheer luck, I had brought Bate to the one place where he might just get the care he needed to survive. Father and daughter stood together over Bate's unconscious form, he giving orders, she following them, only questioning occasionally. The young girl busied herself fetching water and towels and anything else that was required in response to her grandfather's barked instructions. I thought it was best to leave them to it and I sat on an old wooden chair in the corner.

Overwhelmed by exhaustion, I was asleep in moments.

I WAS WOKEN by a hand gently rocking my shoulder. I started awake in alarm, but soon got my bearings. A glass of Calvados was being waved under my nose, so I took it and sank it in one grateful gulp, savouring the burn.

I blinked and rubbed the sleep from my eyes. I ached all over. Looking up, I saw that I had been woken by Madame Defarge, who took the empty glass from me.

'Bonne matin,' she said sarcastically.

With the shutters all closed it was impossible to tell whether it was night or day outside.

'How long was I asleep?' I asked.

'Only an hour,' she replied, moving to stand by the kitchen table on which Bate lay, naked from the waist up, his shoulder swathed in bandages. I was relieved to see that he was still breathing. The old man and the young girl were also sitting at the table, both looking weary.

'How is he?' I asked.

'We cleaned the wound, set the collarbone and stitched him closed. But he has lost a lot of blood. My father thinks he will survive, but it is not certain. He should sleep now, in one of the beds upstairs, but I will need your help to carry him.'

'Of course,' I said, rising from the chair. 'Thank you for all you've done.'

I moved to the head of the table and wrapped my arms around his chest, careful not to disturb his collarbone, while Madame Defarge took his feet. He was a dead weight, but we managed to manoeuvre him out of the kitchen into a stone-flagged hallway that led to the main door of the house. The staircase was wider than I had expected, and it was relatively easy to carry our patient upstairs.

'Left,' said Madame Defarge when we reached the top, and I hefted my friend through a doorway into a large bedroom. It was simply furnished with a wooden cupboard and a large metal bed frame. We lowered Bate gently onto the bed and Madame Defarge pulled a blanket over him.

I halfheartedly attempted to fix his brylcreemed hair, now full of dirt and twigs, but it was hopeless. He'd be horrified when he woke.

'There is nothing else we can do,' she said, matter of fact. 'Either he will wake, or he will not.'

'If it's not rude to ask, where is your daughter's father?'

She hung her head. 'I do not know. He was with the army at the front. I have heard nothing. Either he will return or...' She looked up and shrugged.

'Is she your only child?'

She shook her head. 'No, she has an older sister. Much older. She is married. She lives in Paris, but the last I heard her husband had left to join the fight and she was stuck alone in a city that will soon be crawling with Germans. I used to chide her for not giving me a grandchild yet. Now I am grateful she is childless, for it is one less person for me to be afraid for. There is nothing I can do for my daughters except worry every day.'

She left the room without another word and I followed her back downstairs to the kitchen.

'So, Monsieur Américain,' she said when we were sat back in the kitchen. 'Tell us what is happening outside.'

'Well, the Germans have taken the town and captured the men I was fighting with.'

Madame Defarge translated my words for her daughter and father, who both sat silent as I talked.

'There is smoke drifting over the house. Is the town destroyed?'

I shook my head. 'That was the barges. We burnt them to stop the Germans using them as a way across the water. There's a wrecked tank blocking the bridge, so for now they cannot easily advance this way.'

The old man cursed and waved his stick at me as he unleashed a stream of angry French.

'My father says you should have stayed out of it. Soon there will be a jam of German soldiers and vehicles trailing back down the road from the bridge. They will come hunting for food and they will find us. If the bridge was clear, they would have simply passed through, but now we are are in much greater danger because of what you have done.'

My heart sank as I realised Madame Defarge was right. Strategically, we had done the right thing, but as always in war the safety of innocents was the first thing to go out the window.

'What will happen to your fellow soldiers?' she asked.

I shrugged. 'According to the rules of war, they should be taken to an internment camp of some kind.'

She picked up on the doubt in my voice. 'But you do not think they will be so lucky?'

I shook my head. 'These soldiers are SS, not regular army. We've heard rumours of massacres during their advance, so no, I don't trust them. Are you sure you have to stay here? There's nowhere else you can go?'

She scoffed. 'My father can hardly walk, and my daughter has asthma. We have no choice but to stay here. And now you say there are SS wandering around.' She shook her head, despairing. 'Anyway, your friend upstairs is not going anywhere for a long time.'

She shook her shoulders as if banishing her thoughts and rose from her chair. 'I will feed you,' she said. 'You are no use to anybody like this.'

While she busied herself in the pantry, the old man leaned forward and spoke to me in faltering English.

'Last war, I fight Bosche,' he said, his voice dry and brittle as old paper. 'Now they back.' His face was a mask of disgust.

'You won, though. Eventually. Any advice for me?'

The man shrugged, then after a moment's thought, he said, 'Not dig trenches. Trenches are death. Always move. Not stay in one place. Move and fight.'

He did not, could not, know what was happening outside his small farm. To dig trenches, we would have to halt their advance and reach a stalemate. But the blitzkrieg tactics of the German army, their tanks and air superiority, made them unstoppable. There would be no hundred-mile trenches in this war, of that I was certain. The Germans had all the advantage, and they would drive us into the sea. I didn't see how they could lose, but I did not share my dark conclusion with the old man.

Madame Defarge put a plate in front of me. There was half a baguette, some cheese and ham and a glass of water. It seemed like a feast to me at the time, and I wolfed it down as fast as I could. When I was finished, I could feel the strength returning to my aching limbs.

'I should go,' I said, rising from the chair. 'You've risked enough. You, and Bate, will stand more chance without me around. Hide his uniform and if the Germans come and ask, tell them he is an idiot farmhand who injured himself in the fields. They may buy it. Meanwhile, the best thing I can do for you all is to get far away from here.'

None of them rushed to contradict me, so I picked up my pack and walked to the door.

'If I can, I'll come back for him. If not...' I shrugged. Assuming Bate recovered, he would be behind enemy lines. He would have to either surrender, and risk being shot as a spy, or try to make his way home again. Resolving that, if I survived the day, I would return for him by hook or by crook, I put my hand on the door handle.

'Monsieur Américain.'

I turned and looked back at Madame Defarge, standing defiant; her daughter, small and nervous;

her father, old and frail. It was the little girl who had spoken.

'Yes?'

'Kill Bosche,' she said quietly. 'Kill all Bosche.'

I paused, surprised by her cold entreaty.

'I will do my best,' I said and smiled at her in what I hoped was a reassuring manner. She did not return the smile.

8: The Rifle

IT WAS DUSK as I stepped out of the house back into the woods. The half-light lengthened the shadows of the trees and it only took me a few steps into the forest before the night wrapped around me and hid me from view.

My plan was simple. I would find the dead sniper, claim his rifle, and with the scope I would find the SS and observe what was happening to my unit. Assuming, that is, they were still alive. I banished that grim thought and made my way through the darkness. With every step I expected to hear noises of activity coming from ahead, but the night was still and quiet and when I reached the road into town it was deserted. Either the main force was still some way distant, or they had rerouted when they heard the way was blocked. So I still had time.

Even so, the four dead men we had left by the bridge would surely have been found by now. The SS would know that at least one soldier was at large, and they would be watchful. It occurred to me for the first time that maybe they had taken reprisals on the men they were holding. I shuddered at the thought that my actions could have led to the deaths of some or all of my comrades, but I could not let it distract me from my mission.

I crossed the road and entered the woods on the other side. Now I was the right side of the road all I would have to do was work my way slowly and quietly towards the town. It would be difficult to find a single corpse in these woods in the pitch dark, but it was the only thing I could think to do so I pushed on.

Half an hour later I could see the hint of lights through the trees. Night had truly fallen now. I had heard nothing to indicate sentries or hunters, but I had to assume that any noise or mistake on my part would bring them hurrying to my position. I slowed my pace even more, stepping slowly and carefully, inching my way towards danger.

When I reached the treeline, I stayed in the shadows and looked across the canal into the town. There were lights on in a couple of the houses, but all seemed quiet. I was unsure what to do. Had they moved on and left the town to its inhabitants?

First things first—find the rifle.

I judged myself to be about one hundred metres from the bridge, which meant that, by my reckoning, the sniper should be fifty meters to my right and about ten metres inside the treeline. I traced a path towards where I thought he might lie and in the end I found him with little difficulty, but of his rifle there was no sign. At first, I thought it had been taken, but then I glanced upwards and caught a glimpse of something hanging down from an upper branch, framed against the dim town lights.

I didn't fancy trying to climb the tree in the dark. I reluctantly decided I would have to wait for dawn before retrieving it.

I had only searched the sniper in a cursory manner earlier, so I took the opportunity to properly rifle through his pockets and pack. I found a packet of letters, probably from a wife or sweetheart, but I didn't read them. Some cigarettes, but I didn't smoke. Some Pervitin pills, but I had no intention of getting myself addicted to methamphetamine. He had a Luger, which I appropriated; it felt good to have a sidearm again. Finally, there was a bar of dark chocolate, which I ate, and a hipflask of Schnapps, which I drank. Then I curled up under a nearby bush and got some shuteye.

THE LOUD SNAP of a breaking twig startled me awake. The first hints of dawn were creeping through the trees and someone was close. I lay still, breathing as softly as I could, waiting for another sound to reveal the location of the man. A rustle of leaves, the brush of a branch against an arm; he was moving slowly, hunting, and he was about two meters away, just behind the next tree.

I carefully moved my arm down to my belt and grasped the hilt of my knife. If I moved, I had better move either fast, or very, very slow. Ambush him, or emerge when he was past me, and creep up behind him? I decided stealth was the best option.

I saw a pair of muddy boots emerge from behind the tree, walking away from the bridge, searching the woods. Where there was one man, I had to assume there would be more. I had just decided that it would be wiser to wait when I heard the man give a soft exclamation and begin to move quickly.

Dammit, he'd seen the sniper's corpse. If he raised the alarm, there'd be men all over me in seconds. As quietly as I could, I crawled out of my hiding place and circled the tree, coming up behind the man, who was now kneeling over the dead sniper. He never heard me, and my knife had slit his vocal cords before he could raise the alarm. I gently laid his body down on top of the sniper and considered my options. I could now hear other soldiers working their way through the woods in search of me. If I climbed the tree to retrieve the rifle, I would probably alert them. And even if I got up there without giving myself away, if someone found the bodies while I was up there, they would only have to look up and I'd be a dead man.

There was nothing for it: the rifle would have to wait until the search party had moved on. I waited patiently until the noise of the searchers had passed and faded, then I scrambled up the tree as fast as I could, careful to stay as quiet as possible. I eventually reached the rifle, which dangled from a branch by its strap. I gingerly unhooked it, slung it over my back and descended.

Safe on the ground, I searched the dead soldier I had just dispatched and pocketed some ammunition and more chocolate, then I hurried away from the bodies, towards the road, in the opposite direction of the searching soldiers. When I judged myself safe for the moment, I examined the rifle I had claimed.

It was a K98K Mauser, the standard rifle issued to the German army. It was a familiar rifle; I had fired one before during training and admired its simplicity, robustness and accuracy. This one had a sight fitted, the first I had ever seen. I held it up to my eye and was gratified that the glass was unbroken and provided a clear image, many times magnified. The sight was not the only peculiarity—stamped on the left side of the barrel immediately ahead of the receiver was a death's head symbol, the mark of the SS.

I lifted it to my shoulder, dug the stock in, held it steady, sighted through the scope, felt the weight of it, the balance, the stability. It felt good. And something happened to me as I sat there, aiming at nothing. I felt a sense of calm overcome me.

Ever since the fighting had begun, I had been retreating from the enemy amongst men who neither liked nor trusted me. I had felt like an outsider but worse, I had felt useless, as if nothing I did could make a real difference. But as I held that rifle set to fire, I felt in control for the first time in as long as I could remember. I liked Bate, but he had slowed me down. I was better alone. And with a gun like this I could make a difference: fight the war on my own terms, in my own way.

I slung the rifle back over my shoulder, left my Lee Enfield on the forest floor, and moved on towards the town in search of prey.

9: The Rescue

THE TOWN WAS deserted.

The tank still blocked the bridge, but the two trucks that had tried to move it were gone. Taking cover behind the wreckage, I raised the scope to my eye and scanned the town. There was no sign of movement at all, neither occupiers nor inhabitants. The enemy were still searching the woods on this side of the water, presumably for me and Bate, but it seemed the town was no longer a strategic priority. I watched for twenty minutes and finally decided to risk it. I walked across the bridge into Brasee.

The gun emplacements that we had erected stood silent and abandoned. Smoke still wafted out of some of the buildings on Main Street, but none had fully caught fire. They were pockmarked with holes from the firefight, and there wasn't a single window left intact, but there was only silence here.

I entered the building where Bate and I had taken

shelter the day before, intending to collect the dog tags from the soldier who had died in front of us. The body was gone. That stuck me as odd and increased the nagging sense of unease that I couldn't shake. I searched with more and more urgency, always afraid that I would round a corner and find a pile of bodies where the SS had lined my unit up against a wall and shot them. But I found no bodies at all, neither British nor German.

So where was everyone?

They couldn't have advanced through the town, so the only thing that made sense was that they had retreated back the way they had come. Maybe they would go back to some road that ran parallel to the canal and push along it in search of another crossing place. But if that was what they were doing, they would be unlikely to let prisoners slow them down.

I had a sudden apprehension of imminent danger and ran for the bridge, reckless in my haste. As I neared it, a group of SS emerged from the woods on the road beyond the tank. I skidded to a halt but it was too late: they had seen me. A cry went up and I ducked down and scurried to the machine gun nest I had occupied the day before as bullets began to whizz through the air around me.

Taking cover with my back against the sandbags, I had to think quickly. I heard soft metallic clangs and realised they were clambering over the tank onto the bridge. I turned, grabbed the Bren gun and rose from cover, firing. My aim was not true, and I sprayed bullets in a rising arc from the waterline up across the stone abutment on the opposite bank; a terrible, panic-driven arc.

But by sheer fluke one of the bullets hit the explosives that the sappers had been setting beneath the bridge, and with a huge explosion, the far side of the bridge disintegrated.

Flung backwards by the blast, I was showered with fragments of stones, with a large chunk slamming into the ground by my head. When the stone rain had ceased to fall, I pushed myself upright and peered through the dust at what was left. As the smoke cleared I saw the tank slowly topple forwards into the water. Of the men who had been moving to attack me, there was no sign. Figuring it was now or never, I ran fast onto the half of the bridge that was left and leapt onto the small portion of the tank that was sticking up out of the canal. I clambered up it onto the road, and scuttled into the cover of the trees as fast as I could.

I heard shouts in German from all around me as men hurried towards the bridge, drawn by the sound of the explosion. I took cover in some undergrowth and waited for the soldiers to pass me by, then struck out away from the canal as quietly as possible, alert for more movement around me. If any men from my unit were still alive, they were not in the town or the woods. I needed to get to the fields beyond, maybe then I could pick up their tracks.

I moved as quickly as I could without making the kind of noise that would draw attention. Soon I came upon the track that led to the Defarge farm. To my horror, there were fresh tire tracks in the mud. I turned and, keeping within the trees, made haste towards the farmhouse.

As I came closer I could hear German voices. I crept forward slowly, careful to stay in the shadows, until I could see beyond the treeline. Outside the farmhouse stood one of the SS trucks, and beside it were two troopers. They were discussing the big bang they had just heard and wondering whether to inform their superior officer. So that meant wherever their boss was, he was out of earshot. Good to know. I pondered my next move. I was within twenty meters of them, so I could pick them off with the rifle easily but the noise would attract attention. I wasn't sure I wanted to go loud just yet, not until I knew the full situation.

I slowly crawled backwards, deeper into the trees, and skirted around the house, moving forward again to check the far side. Here there were no sentries, so I crept out of cover and up to the side of the building. The shutters were open now, but I could hear nothing from inside. I peered cautiously over the window sill. I was looking into the parlour of the house but the interior doors were open, so I could see through the hallway and into the kitchen beyond.

My view was limited, but through the doorway I saw an SS officer pacing back and forth just inside the room. He had a gun in his hand, but it was not raised. Beyond, at the kitchen table at which I had so recently eaten, I could see the back of the old man. Beyond that, I could not see if Madame Defarge, her daughter or Bate were in there too. I needed to get closer if I was to hear what was going on, but it was too risky. As I sat there wondering what to do next, I caught a flash of movement out of the corner of my eye; there was something happening in the beet-field over by the farmhouse. I turned and raised the scope to my eye. What I saw made my blood run cold.

In the middle of the field stood ten British soldiers. I recognised them as being from my rag-tag unit, so I figured they were all that had survived. They were lined up, each with a shovel in their hands, and they were digging a pit. There were seven SS guards standing around them as they dug, each with a submachine gun in hand. Beside the pit was a pile of bodies. Judging by the uniforms it was a mixture of maybe twenty or so British and German casualties.

So there were seven in the field, two outside the house, and at least one inside the house—probably more. And once I started shooting it was only a matter of time before the soldiers I had left by the bridge came to see what the fuss was about. The odds were not great. If I was to survive this, I would have to be smart.

I decided to begin with the house.

Ducking back down, I crawled to the back of the house. There was a small window here, leading into a simple scullery that sat alongside the kitchen. I had registered that the window was open when I was here earlier, and I was happy to see that it still was. I peered over the sill and was again relieved to see that the door was closed. This was my way in. Climbing through a small window without making a noise was not a simple task; doing it in full combat gear was impossible. I carefully took off my pack and belt, laid down my rifle and rolled up my sleeves. All I needed for this part was my knife. I grasped the sill and pulled myself up and over into the room, moving as slowly and carefully as I could. There was a large metal sink beneath the window, lined in lead, which gave me a good step down into the small room.

Crouching inside the door, I listened to the noises from the kitchen.

'...is wearing thin,' the German officer was saying. 'I do not believe that the man upstairs is any relative of yours. I do not believe he was injured in a farming accident. How stupid you must think me. This is the last time I shall ask: I want to know who brought him here? How long ago? Where did they go?'

'Monsieur,' replied the old man, his voice barely audible through the wood. 'We do not know what...'

But his voice was cut short by the sudden report of a handgun, a moment of shocked silence, and then a piercing scream. My stomach sank. If only I had moved more quickly. As Madame Defarge screamed I took a chance and turned the door handle, cracking it open just slightly. The old man was lying, slumped forward cross the table with his back to me. I could see blood pooling on the wood and trickling off the table onto the floor. Standing over him, his gun raised and pointed at the young girl's head, was the officer.

Madame Defarge was kneeling beside her daughter on the opposite side to me, clinging onto her, while the girl stared defiantly up into the officer's face. Taking advantage of the screaming I stood upright, pushed open the door, stepped forward quickly, and, with the ease of an action many times rehearsed, sealed the officer's mouth with my left hand while I slit his throat to the bone with the knife in my right. This time I was prepared for the shift of his weight and I gently lowered him as his mouth moved silently and the last air gurgled up out of his severed windpipe. He was dead before I laid him down.

Madame Defarge stopped screaming and stared at me, shocked and wide-eyed. The young girl just smiled. She was kind of terrifying.

I bent down and picked up the officer's Luger.

'Still got my gun?' I asked.

Madame Defarge shook her head and pointed to the officer. I searched his pockets and found the Webley, which I handed to Madame Defarge. I gestured for her to stand behind the outside door, and when she had taken up position—still mute, still in shock—I took up post on the other side. Then I cracked the door open and barked in German, imitating the high, nasal voice of the man dead on the floor: 'In here, quickly!'

I leant back behind the door and within moments the two soldiers who had been standing by the truck outside came hurrying into the room. I stepped forward and placed the muzzle of the Luger at the base of the neck of the one closest to me. Madame Defarge did the same with the man closest to her.

'Drop the guns!' I barked in German. Both men did so.

'Fetch bedsheets,' said Madame Defarge to her daughter who, still smiling, ran upstairs to get linens which which to bind and gag our captives.

'On the floor, face down, hands behind your heads,' I said, and the men complied.

The girl returned, and together we ripped the sheets into strips and tied the men up.

'Is that all of them?' I asked, when we were done.

Madame Defarge nodded.

'Stay here and lock the door. Don't open it for anyone but me, understand?'

She nodded again and I snuck out the door, keeping close to the wall of the house, heading to the back and redonning my kit.

Now to deal with the men in the field. But before I could take up position, I heard gunfire.

10: The Sniper

I RACED AROUND the house and hurried to the low stone
wall that ringed the property. I chambered a round in
my rifle as I ran, and as soon as I reached the wall I
knelt down, put my arms on the wall, raised the rifle
to my shoulder, put my eye to the scope and sighted.

To my immense relief the captive British soldiers
were still alive. They were, however, still standing in
the pit. They had stopped digging and were all staring
up at one of their guards in fear. There was smoke still
curling from the muzzle of his machine gun. It looked
as if he had fired to get their attention. The guard
next to him was laughing at the effect it had had on
the captives.

Although I could hear the orders he barked, he was
too far away for me to hear the exact words. The
captives let go of their shovels. One crossed himself.
Another fell to his knees. I saw Blaster there, standing
tall, staring defiantly into the face of the guard who

was shouting at them; I finally felt a tiny bit of respect for him at that moment.

I breathed out and caressed the trigger with my right index finger. It was clear what was about to happen, and I would not allow it. I focused my attention on the guard who had been laughing, moving the crosshairs of the sight up his body until I centred on his heart. I did not yet know how to adjust this weapon to compensate for distance and crosswind, so centre mass was my best bet of a hit. I reckoned they were one hundred and fifty meters away, and there was only a light breeze. I had always been a good marksman, so this should be pretty easy.

The guards all raised their machine guns. I gently squeezed the trigger.

And missed.

I saw my target start and look to his left in alarm as the sound of my shot reached him, so I quickly pulled the crosshairs a foot to the right of his heart, chambered another round and fired again. This shot landed true, straight through the heart. The SS soldier jerked backwards and fell, arms outstretched, gun falling to the ground, an arc of blood spraying out behind him as he toppled.

Two bullets down, three to go before I would have to reload, six men to kill, ten men to save.

I sighted on the guard who had fired his gun. He was turning, alarmed, raising his gun but unsure where to point it. He ducked slightly, as if that would provide any cover. I chambered another round, breathed out, sighted again, being sure to pull the crosshairs to the right. Squeeze, fire.

The bullet took him in the chest and he fell backwards, crumbling as he collapsed, folding in two and slumping to the ground as if he'd sat down violently. He lay there, bent over, head lolling forward, twitching as his muscles spasmed. It looked like he was crying.

So far it had been about seven seconds since my first shot.

The five SS men who remained were reacting to my attack in different ways. One was running for the road. I was happy to let him go; one less bullet to waste. Two more were running towards the pile of corpses that lay at the side of the pit, intending to take cover behind dead flesh. One was just standing there looking surprised. The final man was jumping down into the pit with my comrades; he was going to be a problem.

First things first, though. I sighted on the startled one, chambered the fourth round, breathed out, sighted in on him. He was immobile, frozen. It felt too easy. But it also gave me an opportunity to try for a more precise shot. So I aimed a foot to the side of his stupid, goggle-eyed, dumbfounded face and put a bullet right between his eyes.

I didn't even watch him fall, because I was chambering the final round of this clip and moving my sight down to the pit, searching for the SS soldier who was sheltering amongst the captives.

There was confusion in the pit, a struggle, a mess of moving people. I couldn't find a target. Then a burst of gunfire from behind the pile of corpses and some shouts. Everyone in the pit froze. Dammit. The two men hiding behind the bodies, who I had no line of sight on, had a clear line of fire towards the captives in the pit. I had been outfoxed. Stupid.

I cursed. But there was an upside to this temporary stalemate. I turned and crouched down behind the wall, taking a moment to refill the clip on the rifle. My hands were shaking, and I dropped a few rounds, but eventually I slammed the full clip back into the rifle. With one round in the chamber, I had six shots. I crawled quickly behind the wall, changing my position, making it harder for them to get a bead on me. Then I took a deep breath, spun and rose to firing position.

My fellow soldiers were out of the pit now, moving en masse towards the road. The three remaining SS men were in amongst them, guns raised, using them as a human shield. As soon as they reached the road, and the trees beyond it, they would flee, but not before, inevitably, killing all the captives. I had, I reckoned, about forty meters to finish this once and for all.

I sighted in on the group.

One of the SS men had a Luger to the head of one of the captives—Blaster. They were in the middle of the group, which was moving slowly. Another SS man was tightly encircled by three men and had his machine gun raised. I couldn't find the third, and assumed he was crouched behind the group, covering them as they retreated. I figured if I shot two of them, the men would have a chance to overwhelm and disarm the third.

But who to take first? And did I dare take a shot at a moving target, only partially visible, in amongst the very men whose lives I was trying to save? A few centimetres one way or the other and I could be blowing the wrong brains out. That made the choice easier—I decided to take out the guy with his gun to Blaster's head.

Only half his face was visible, and he was moving side to side as he walked, kind of weaving, as if to make my job harder. This was not going to be easy. I breathed out, sighted on Blaster's head and held my aim steady. Rather than trying to move the rifle to track my target, I was sighting on a specific spot and waiting for him to weave into my line of fire. I waited as he moved, getting a sense of his rhythm and speed. One, two, three... I fired.

The top of his head came clean off and Blaster disappeared from view, pulled down by the tumbling corpse that entwined with him. I knew that things would move quickly and unpredictably now, so I pulled back the bolt and chambered another round as quickly as I could.

The SS man who had built a little shield around himself with three men was wild-eyed and panicking. His movements were too erratic for me to get a clean shot. Then I saw one of the British soldiers mouthing something in an exaggerated fashion. I focused on him. It took me a few moments to realise he was counting down... for me!

As he reached one, he dropped, leaving his captor suddenly exposed. I took him easily, blowing his left lung out of his back.

And then there was one. I pulled back the bolt and loaded another bullet. But there was a commotion in the group. They had all turned their backs to me and were crowding in together. There was a burst of machine gun fire and I gasped in alarm. But then a cheer went up and I realised they had taken care of the final SS man themselves.

I breathed out, relieved, and rose from concealment, waving to them as I vaulted the wall and walked across the field towards them.

Epilogue

THE WINE IS flowing, and the old soldier is feeling a pleasant warmth as the alcohol soothes away the aches and pains of old wounds.

Madame Defarge, white-haired now but still with a sparkle in her eye, is sitting at the head of the table, laughing. She has insisted that he call her Dominique.

Her youngest daughter, Yvette, sits beside her, a sardonic smile the extent of her merriment. To her right is Dominique's eldest daughter, Marie. The old soldier wonders at the coincidence that has brought them together again. When they fought together in 1944, during the dark days of Operation Kraken, he had no idea that she was the child of the woman who had saved his life, and whose life he had saved in turn, back in 1940. Marie's husband, Claude, sits beside her, and on his lap is their son, Bernard.

It is rare for him to feel contentment, but the warmth of their welcome, the place they have given him at their family table, has brought the old soldier a moment of peace.

As he leans forward to take another slice of bread, there is a knock at the door.

'Aha! The last of our party!' Dominique rises and goes to open the door.

It takes the old soldier a moment to make out the face of the man who enters and steps slowly into the glow of the candlelight, but when the features solidify, he smiles broadly and rises to greet an old friend.

Karl Fairburne embraces Albert Bate in the house where they last saw each other so many years before, and then they sit with their French friends and drink wine, and share stories, and laugh long until the sun creeps over the horizon.

Afterword

In May 1940 my grandfather, Gunner Albert Bate of the Royal Engineers, was part of the desperate retreat of the British Expeditionary Force to Dunkirk. A career soldier, he was a radio operator at this point. He died when I was twelve, so I never got to talk to him as an adult, to ask about his life and his experiences of the war, but one story has been passed down to me.

At some point during the retreat, he and a friend were captured by German forces. Somehow, they managed to escape and sought refuge with a French family who, at great risk to themselves, hid them from the Germans. Eventually, when the search had passed them by, my grandfather and his friend made a break for it and were able to rejoin the BEF, eventually being evacuated from the beach at Dunkirk.

I have an old photo of my grandfather in his army fatigues, sitting happily surrounded by a large family. I think it was taken in 1944 when he was part of the push towards Berlin, retracing his steps of four years previously, this time in the opposite direction. During this time he managed to revisit the family who had saved his life, and the photo records that reunion.

He returned to visit them many times in the years after the war.

This little story is for him, and for them, because without their bravery I would not be here to write it.

HOME GROUND
by Sandy Mitchell

ONE

Colline Sur Mer, Occupied France, 1944

BY THAT POINT in the war I'd long given up on being surprised, but stumbling across an old friend in the middle of a sabotage operation behind enemy lines came as close to it as I'd felt in quite a while. But it did make an odd kind of sense. While we'd been training together she'd been expecting to work in occupied France, helping the Resistance to raise as much hell as they could: which, for Charlie Barton, was a heck of a lot.

We should have stuck together, I told myself, ghosting from shadow to shadow among the ruins of Colline Sur Mer. The town was a shattered parody of its former self, buildings collapsed into rubble, fitful fires still smouldering here and there and the charnel stench of bodies left to rot where they'd fallen mingling with the smoke. Savage reprisals for the damage Charlie's resistance cell had inflicted on the German war effort around here.

Which didn't make sense to me. A few hijacked trucks, the odd sentry left dead in a ditch; it wasn't worth slaughtering or driving out hundreds of innocent civilians. There must be something else going on in Colline Sur Mer, something London didn't know about.

If Charlie was here I could simply have asked her what her people had discovered, instead of scuttling around the ruins like a rat hoping to retrieve a bundle of documents one of her cell members had hidden before he died. But after that last skirmish she was too beat up to move as fast or as quietly as I could. Better for both of us if she headed for the safe house while I did the leg work, and we met up again after I'd got hold of the papers.

The scrape of boot soles against pavement and the faint clatter of dislodged rubble warned me that I had company, and I melted into the doorway of a reasonably intact cafe. The smell of spilled alcohol mingled with the pervasive charnel odour, hinting that at least some of the Nazi butchers had helped themselves to its contents: an impression confirmed by the shattered remains of the door.

I moved inside cautiously, allowing my eyes to adjust to the faint, flickering illumination from a nearby fire which struck in through the now-glassless window. I eased the Lee Enfield from my back and waited, my eyes on the door, taking in my surroundings. Most of the tables and chairs were intact, though disarrayed, a few of them still bearing glasses and bottles. The bar was made of polished wood, marred with dark stains, the bottles behind it mostly missing; an indistinct mass huddled in front of it was all that was left of the owner. As my eyes acclimatised to the deeper gloom of the cafe's interior, I began to make out other victims of the Nazi savagery, though whether they had been staff or customers I had no clue.

I strained my ears, listening for some indication of who might be approaching. Charlie and I had left no one alive enough to raise an alarm, but it could only be a matter of time before someone discovered the bodies. The bombing raid the RAF had laid on just up the coast would be diverting most of the local garrison's attention, as intended, but that wouldn't last for much longer; the muffled crump of distant detonation was already lessening in its intensity.

'Complete waste of time,' a voice said in German, the tone bored and resentful. 'The resistance rats were all rounded up days ago.'

'And any who weren't will be long gone,' another agreed. Shadows moved beyond the door, then the flare of a match briefly illuminated two men, their black SS uniforms rendering them almost invisible in the darkness. Helpful of them, then, to mark their positions with the faint red glow of cigarettes. They must have been as confident of their safety as they sounded, or they'd never have dared strike a light where a well-concealed sniper might see it. But then they had no reason to suspect the presence of an enemy, particularly one as close as I was.

I raised the rifle, aiming carefully at the nearest through the telescopic sight which, at this distance, rendered him inhumanly large, almost impossible to miss. I say almost, because you can never take a shot for granted, but squeezing the trigger at this range would have been shooting a very big fish in a very small barrel.

I stilled my breath, assessing the situation. If I dropped him, I'd have a fraction of a second to switch aim to his companion before he realised what was happening and reacted. I was confident I could do it; both men carried their machine pistols slung, a piece of carelessness which would have earned them the chewing out of a lifetime from any competent officer who saw them, but pretty much a gift to me—by the time either of them got their weapons ready they'd both be long past any hope of using them.

Better to wait, though. Chances were they'd both move off in a moment, continuing their desultory sweep of the town; why risk attracting attention with the sound of gunshots?

After a tense couple of minutes I realised I'd made the right call. The two men flicked their cigarette butts away, and prepared to move out. I kept the rifle aimed, though, bracketing the door. I wouldn't relax until I heard their footsteps fading.

'Just a minute.' One of the shadows took a step closer to the doorway, and my finger tightened incrementally on the trigger. Then I realised he was fumbling with his fly buttons, and eased the pressure off. 'Too much coffee.'

'I don't know how you can stomach that ersatz schisse.'

The figure in the doorway shrugged. 'Got to drink something. When was the last time you saw any of the real stuff?' Then he stopped, bringing his head up to stare into the bar. I remained motionless, acutely aware that the slightest movement could betray my position. 'Someone's in there!'

'Like hell they are.' His companion sounded distinctly unconvinced, but I heard the faint rustle of the weapon sling slipping off his shoulder, followed by the clack of a round being chambered. 'Probably just rats. There's enough carrion in there to attract them.'

'Rats don't wear boots.' The man in the doorway began to unsling his own weapon.

He never completed the movement. At such a short range the bullet from my Lee Enfield struck him almost instantaneously, blowing most of his brains out through the back of his skull. He pitched backwards, his corpse blocking the door. Not that I'd have made a break for it with his friend sheltering behind the wall, waiting to gun me down the moment I moved into the open, anyway.

I swore quietly under my breath, diving to the left as soon as I'd squeezed the trigger, aware that the muzzle flash would have betrayed my position, but fortunately the second man seemed not to have seen inside the room, his view of most of it blocked by the first man until he'd fallen. Rattled by his comrade's sudden demise, he seemed in no hurry to try coming in after me, even without the obstacle of the gently oozing corpse.

I ejected the spent cartridge, chambered another and cast around, looking for some other avenue of escape. The frame of the window facing onto the street was empty, apart from jagged teeth of shattered glass, but trying to get out that way would simply bring me into the line of fire of the hidden enemy. My only chance was to get behind the bar, and hope there was a back way out. And if there wasn't, at least it offered some relatively solid cover to get behind while I did my best impression of Custer's last stand.

I crawled quickly across the floor, while my adversary stuck a nervous arm around the door frame and sent a burst of automatic fire ripping through the room. Luckily for me he wasn't aiming and the bullets whined overhead, gouging splinters from the furniture and shattering a few stray bottles. I made it into cover, more by luck than judgement, and rose to a crouch, resting the rifle on the bar counter, sighting carefully on the doorway again. The Nazi had popped back into cover, and I stilled my breathing, waiting for him to peer round the edge to see if he'd got me. But he didn't. The speed and accuracy with which I'd dispatched his friend was inclining him to caution, and I could hardly blame him for that.

Even as I curled my finger round the trigger, I could see that my worst fears had been confirmed. There was no door to a back room here, no trapdoor to a cellar. My only way out was past the stormtrooper, who seemed in no hurry to come out where I could shoot him. And why would he be? It was dollars to doughnuts that someone would have heard the gunfire, and be on their way to investigate. I had to finish this fast, before I became the fish in the barrel.

The movement was so quick, and so low to the floor, that I almost missed it. Something came rattling into the room, bouncing off one of the table legs, and skittering across the polished wooden planks. I just had time to duck below the counter before the grenade exploded, deafening me with the overlapping echoes, the shrapnel slamming into the thick wood of the bar. Dazed, I rose, reaching for the rifle—and found nothing there. The explosion had shaken the whole structure, tipping the weapon forward; as my groping hand tried to close around the butt it slipped away, disappearing over the edge of the counter. I closed my grip convulsively, snagging the shoulder strap, and taking the weight; the rifle dangled uselessly in midair as I dragged it back.

And I looked up to see the enemy soldier framed in the doorway, his sub machine gun levelled, his finger already tightening on the trigger. I had the barest of instants to live: even as I began to duck down again I knew I'd never make it.

Then a pistol barked, twice, taking him in the back. Even as he began to fall I started to move, sprinting round the edge of the bar, towards the shattered window, bringing the rifle up ready to fire. Half the Wermacht in town would have heard the explosion, never mind the gunfire, and I was going to need all my skill at stealth and evasion to complete my mission now.

But at least I was alive enough to continue with it. As I hit the street I caught sight of my rescuer, melting into the shadows of a nearby alley, that flash of blonde hair unmistakable. Charlie, of course. She waved and was gone before I could return the gesture.

But then, she'd had my back for almost as long as I'd known her.

TWO

Glendreich, Scottish Highlands, 1940

No one was waiting on the platform, and no one else got off the train. I swung my suitcase down from the luggage rack and staggered out of the carriage, yawning. A flensing wind smacked me in the face, banishing the last vestiges of sleep. I hadn't intended to doze off on the final leg of the journey, but the trip from London had been a gruelling one, involving several changes of train on to ever slower and less comfortable services, and I'd acquired the knack of resting whenever I could.

The locomotive, a squat black shape in the gathering dusk, hissed impatiently, then chugged away with its retinue of maroon coaches, leaving me standing on the wooden decking, getting my first good look at my surroundings.

Beautiful desolation just about summed it up. The sky was that pearlescent haze you only get in the

Highlands when the light begins to fade, reflecting the silver sheen of the sea loch in the distance. The glittering waves were embraced by rising moorland, green-brown and purple mingling in a breathtaking patchwork with the darker haze of the surrounding mountains hanging like distant clouds on the horizon, as though they might be suddenly dispersed by a breath of wind. The air was clean, apart from the faint, lingering scent of coal smoke from the departed train, already a vapour-wreathed caterpillar fading into the landscape. Clean, and bloody cold.

I dropped my suitcase and blew on my hands, looking around for some signs of life, but there was nothing, unless you counted the faint cries of the raptors wheeling overhead, or the discarded cigarette packet chasing itself in wind-driven circles in one corner of the open-fronted shelter at the far end of the platform. I turned the collar of my coat up, wishing I'd had the foresight not to leave my scarf in the bottom of the case, and pulled my cap low over my eyes. The civilian clothes still felt strange, but my orders had been clear—ditch the uniform. Not that it would have attracted much attention in the early stages of my trip, servicemen were everywhere, but it would have stood out like a sore thumb in the wilds of Glendreich, miles from the nearest garrison.

Or, at least, I suppose it would have done if there was anyone else in sight.

I walked down to the shelter, past the wooden posts which had once held the station sign—even this deep into the boondocks, it seemed, anything that might have helped an invading German army to orientate itself had been removed. A fear that was all too real in southern England, with the victorious Wermacht poised across the channel, close enough to spit at. I'd done a lot more than spit at them before reaching the beach at Dunkirk, but in the end I'd barely made it out, on a fishing boat so dangerously overloaded it almost sank on the way back. If you saw *The Nancy Starling* at the movies, believe me, it was nothing like that. This far north, though, the only German invaders we were likely to see would be coming from Norway, and good luck to them if they tried it—they'd be torpedoed and strafed into oblivion before they got halfway here from Narvik.

The end of the platform wasn't much of an improvement on the middle, but at least there was a path there, if you were prepared to use the word loosely enough. Little more than a line of flattened heather, through which the occasional rock or patch of bare earth was visible, it wound away across the moors in the general direction of nowhere in particular. Just to be sure, I circled back, checking the other side of the station, but there was no other indication that anyone ever came here, so the path it would have to be. Picking up my case again, and hurrying as much as

I dared before I lost the waning light, I set off across the heath, cursing a little under my breath. My orders had been straightforward enough—make my way to the Glendreich training facility, and report in. Well, this was the glen, right enough, but of the SOE camp I could see no sign. Perhaps it was some kind of test. Or an administrative foul-up. Or I'd simply gotten off at the wrong stop, in which case God alone knew where I was.

No point worrying about any of that, though. I'd been in tighter spots in northern France, and at least this time no one was shooting at me. One of the first things I learned at West Point was doing the wrong thing in a crisis was always better than doing nothing at all. So I stumbled on in the increasing darkness, slowing as the light faded; the last thing I needed to do was turn an ankle. In the end I was moving at a snail's pace, testing every footfall before putting my full weight on it. After a while, the sky began to burn, ripples of colour, rich blues, greens and yellows, chasing one another across the firmament. I found I could see a little more clearly - although it took a fair amount of self-control to keep my attention on my feet, rather than look up at the celestial fireworks display.

I was so intent on my careful progress that I hadn't realised I was almost at the end of the path until I glanced up, and froze. I was just below the crest of a ridge, on which an unmistakable human silhouette was standing, swathed in an overcoat and topped with a wide-brimmed hat. Something large and indistinct, a boulder perhaps, was a few yards further on.

I could have called out, I suppose, but something held me back. Paranoia's an asset in my line of work, and there was too much about this situation I didn't like. Instead, I eased my case gently to the ground, suddenly grateful for the springy heather which silently took the weight, and moved forward as stealthily as I could. A weapon would have been comforting, but I didn't really need one—I've been taking care of myself since the bullies at school in Berlin thought the auslander kid would be an easy target, and I showed them how wrong they were.

I went wide, assuming the watcher on the ridge would be paying particular attention to the path, and suddenly found out two interesting things. Firstly, the going underfoot abruptly became firm, a macadamised road, twisting away like a dark river in the glow from the aurora; and, secondly, that the boulder was nothing of the kind. An automobile had been pulled up just off the highway, a nondescript civilian model I probably wouldn't have recognised even in daylight.

'Sod it.' A faint green glow appeared below the left sleeve of the watcher's overcoat, the light of a radium watch dial, and I released an involuntary breath of surprise. The voice was that of a woman. 'Don't tell me he's broken his bloody leg like the last one.' I held my breath, waiting for a reply, but none came. She evidently hadn't been expecting one either, because she emitted a sigh of exasperation, and pulled a heavy flashlight from her pocket. 'Five more minutes, matey, and if I have to come and find you, a compound fracture's going to be the least of your worries.'

'You won't,' I said, striding forward out of the shadows. Clearly this was supposed to be my ride to the camp, wherever that was, and I've always thought it bad manners to keep a lady waiting.

She reacted instantly and without a word, spinning round and swinging the flashlight at my head. I blocked it reflexively, then went down hard, the breath driven from my lungs by a kick to my sternum a mule would have been proud of. The flashlight beam clicked on, spotlighting me as I staggered to my feet.

'That's some kick you've got,' I said, squinting as I tried to make out who'd attacked me. The backwash from the torch picked out a wisp of blonde hair, escaping from beneath the hat, and a wide grin.

'Count yourself lucky,' she said. 'I thought you were taller.' Her eyes narrowed a little as she lowered the torch from my face, taking in every detail of my appearance. 'You are Lieutenant Shafer, I take it?'

'I go by Fairburne,' I said. 'Took Dad's name when Mom remarried.' It wasn't like I remembered Leopold Shafer in any case. I'd been less than a year old when he died. Freddie Fairburne was the only father I'd ever known, and he was a pretty good one all things considered.

'Right.' She nodded, and I was suddenly convinced she'd already known that, and I'd just passed some kind of test. Clearly the world of cloaks and daggers was a lot more complicated than that of a simple soldier. 'But you speak German, I'm told. Still with a Canadian accent?'

'No accent,' I said, 'unless you count native Berliner. And I'm American, not Canadian.'

'Really?' For the first time she looked surprised. 'So what were you doing at Dunkirk?'

'Keeping my head down, mostly,' I said, in no mood to talk about it. She tilted her head quizzically, and I found myself still speaking anyway. Whoever this woman was, she was good at what she did. 'My Mom's British, and I saw for myself what the Nazis are like growing up in Berlin. I couldn't stand by and do nothing.'

'So you resigned your commission in the States and came to England to enlist,' she said, either joining the dots remarkably fast, or recalling a file she'd read. I assumed the latter at the time, but after I'd come to know her a bit better, I was a lot less sure about that. 'That can't have been easy.'

'Having a father in the State Department kind of helped,' I said, smiling at the memory. Neither of my parents had been exactly thrilled at the idea, but fair play to Dad; once he realised how determined I was, he'd smoothed my path as much as he could. Even accepted me dropping out of West Point to do it, despite having told me once that the day I'd been accepted there had been one of the proudest of his life. I shivered, and blew on my hands again. 'Listen, I'm happy to make small talk for as long as you like, but can we do it somewhere a little warmer?'

'By all means.' The woman reached out and opened the car door. 'Do you have any luggage?' She frowned at me. 'If you've left it at the station you can fetch it yourself.'

'One suitcase,' I said. 'Just over there.' I went to collect it, while she kept me centred in the torch beam. When I lifted the bag, she nodded approvingly.

'You travel light, I see. Well done, Lieutenant Fairburne. One chap turned up with a set of golf clubs.'

'Boxing's more my game,' I said, turning back to the car, still squinting a little against the light. 'And my friends call me Karl.'

'Mine call me Charlie. Short for Charlotte.' She clicked the flashlight off and I blinked for a moment, allowing my eyes to adjust to the auroral glow again. 'But you can stick to Miss Barton for now.'

'Delighted to make your acquaintance, Miss Barton,' I said, swinging the bag into the trunk of the car. The strange thing was, I almost meant it.

THREE

I DIDN'T GET to see much of the countryside on the mostly silent drive, apart from the road unwinding in front of us and the indistinct masses of nearby hills in the ever-changing glow of the aurora. Charlie drove fast and without headlights, although I'd seen the blackout masking on them before we set off. Unsure of whether she was trying to gauge my nerve, or simply showing off, I said nothing about it; not least because distracting her seemed a little unwise under the circumstances. Instead, I simply resumed my interrupted nap, rousing only as the car coasted to a halt.

'Sorry if you found the company a bit boring,' Charlie said, as I cranked my eyes open. Her tone was frosty, but her eyes held a glimmer of amusement, so I smiled in response and exaggerated my yawn a little.

'Not at all. It's been a long trip.'

She tilted her head appraisingly. 'The one you go on from here will be a lot longer, believe me.'

'Depends where you think I started out from,' I said.

The corner of her mouth quirked a little. 'I wouldn't care to speculate.' She wound the window down, and I became aware of a shadow moving in the darkness beyond it. I peered through the windshield, but could make out very little apart from a cottage, light leaking around the blackout shutters secured to its windows, and a door, left ajar. As my eyes adjusted to the feeble illumination the shadow resolved itself into a man, middle-aged and heavyset, dressed in tweeds, a double-barrelled shotgun held not quite casually in his right hand. 'Good evening, Lennox.'

'Good morning, more like.' His voice held the distinctive brogue of the Highlands, and he glanced in my direction with mild curiosity. 'This the new one?'

'He is.' Her voice took on a tinge of amusement. 'And he's an American, apparently.'

'Not had one of those before.' Lennox nodded to me. 'But I can't pretend we're not grateful for the help.' He moved away, and began to push an ornate wrought iron gate open. The hinges grated, setting my teeth on edge.

I must have grimaced, because I caught Charlie suppressing what looked a lot like a smirk. She put the car in gear, and we rolled through the gate; beyond it was a long, winding driveway, which led us through a smoother, more managed landscape. An indistinct looming mass in the distance began to resolve itself into an isolated manor house, surrounded by outbuildings like a mother hen with her chicks; as we got nearer, some of them proved to be modern additions—Nissen huts for the most part. I'd spent enough time on British army bases to find the distinctive semicircular silhouettes comfortingly familiar, and felt myself relaxing almost imperceptibly.

'He was chatty,' I said.

Charlie shrugged. 'He must like you. That's the most I've ever heard him say to a new arrival.'

'Can't think why,' I said. 'Is he an officer?'

'He's a civilian. Came with the estate. But he's a good man. Doesn't ask questions.'

'I see.' I nodded, taking the hint, and shut up.

FOUR

THE FIRST FAINT blush of sunrise was beginning to taint the sky as we pulled up outside the house, gravel crunching under the tyres, and I was certain I saw Charlie suppressing a yawn out of the corner of my eye. I popped the door latch, and grinned.

'Not keeping you up, am I?' I asked, with exaggerated concern. 'Or is the company a little dull?'

'Both.' But the smile was hovering just behind her eyes again. 'Don't forget your case.'

'Wasn't planning to,' I said. I walked round behind the car, and opened the trunk. As I lifted my luggage out it bumped against something: a Thompson submachine gun, tucked into the tool well where the lug wrench should have been. If I'd realised it was there, I wouldn't have thrown my suitcase in quite so casually. I closed the trunk carefully. 'Do you have much use for the tool kit?'

'Haven't needed it yet,' Charlie said. 'But you can't

be too careful. Lot of disreputable types around these days.' Then she gunned the engine and took off in a spray of stinging gravel, which I strongly suspected had been entirely for my benefit.

I looked around. The camp was beginning to come to life, with men and a few women in British battledress devoid of insignia appearing from hut doors and going about their business, most of them with no more than a glance in my direction. I was clearly far from the first new recruit they'd seen, and none of them seemed any more interested in me than Lennox had been. I suppose I could have hailed one of the passersby and asked for directions, but finding my way to the rendezvous with Charlie had obviously been some kind of test, and I was loath to flunk one after having passed the first. So, instead, I just walked up the steps to the front door of the house, and pushed it open.

I'd half-expected it to be locked, but the handle gave as soon as I turned it and the huge slab of oak swung smoothly aside on well-oiled hinges. Something like that should have groaned like the castle door in a Bela Lugosi flick, but it was almost silent, emitting no more than the faintest of squeaks, like an excessively polite mouse trying to attract a waiter's attention. My footsteps rang on a stone-flagged floor, rendered slightly uneven by generations of wear. Faint footfall-worn grooves marked the most frequent journeys between the front door and the rooms leading off on either side. Immediately opposite the main entrance was a staircase wide enough to have ridden a horse up, rising to a landing where it bifurcated, splitting off to the right and left. A number of paintings of people in old-fashioned clothes, so grubby and faded that they were barely visible, clung to the walls in weary resignation; and a suit of armour, so impractical and historically inaccurate it could only have been a Victorian reproduction, stood guard over the staircase landing.

'You must be Fairburne,' a voice said, and a tall man in a well-fitting uniform devoid of insignia unfolded himself from an armchair in the alcove beneath the left-hand branch of the staircase. He had a newspaper in his left hand, folded several times to allow easy access to the crossword, and tucked a pencil into his breast pocket as he stood. He held out his right hand, now free, and I shook it, after hastily shifting my suitcase to the other side. 'I'm Major Protheroe, the officer in charge of this little circus.'

'Sir.' I dropped the case and snapped to attention, with one of my best parade-ground salutes. I should have realised he outranked me. Hardly the impression I'd hoped to make on my arrival.

Protheroe smiled and indicated the alcove, where another chair waited opposite the one he'd occupied. 'No need for that. You'll find we dispense with the niceties around here. All in the same boat, what?' He dropped back into his old seat. 'We take all sorts. Not all of them particularly military in their outlook, if you see what I mean.'

'I think I do,' I said, settling into the other. 'Your driver's definitely on the unconventional side.'

'Better not let her hear you calling her that,' Protheroe said, with a snort of barely suppressed amusement. 'Miss Barton's one of our most promising trainees. F Section will be lucky to have her.'

'She's a field agent?' I asked, although after what I'd seen of her I hardly found that surprising.

Protheroe nodded. 'She will be, once we've decided where she can do the most good. Given her particular set of skills, that might take a while.'

'She seems capable of taking care of herself,' I conceded, and Protheroe nodded again.

'She can, and she speaks French like a native. Rather like your German, she picked it up living there as a child. Both of you could pass for locals, which might come in handy when the right assignment comes along.'

'I think there's been some kind of mistake,' I said. 'I'm not cut out for that John Buchan stuff. I'm a soldier, pure and simple.'

'Don't sell yourself short.' Protheroe looked at me appraisingly. 'You're here because you're clearly something far more than that. A plain, simple soldier couldn't have done what you did in London.'

I shrugged, unable to meet his eye. 'I just did what anyone would have done under those circumstances.'

'Maybe you did, but I doubt very much that anyone else could have survived them. And you have the gratitude of the Prime Minister, which is usually something to be wary of.' The major had a hint of amusement in his eye. 'Anyway, he seems to think you have potential. What kind is for us to find out, and hone.'

I shrugged. 'I'm pretty good at shooting stuff. And I've a fair right hook. I think that about covers it.'

'There you go again, underestimating yourself.' Protheroe smiled indulgently. 'But the Special Operations Executive has a knack for collecting square pegs, and finding the right hole for them. Whether that's sabotage, espionage, or simple assassination, whatever we find you're good at, we'll be able to use.'

'Well, that's good enough for me,' I said, despite the doubts I felt. I'd done all right working on my own in northern France, harassing the advancing Wermacht and buying what time I could for my comrades to reach the beaches, but part of me had missed being in a unit, knowing my squad mates would have my back. On the other hand, I'd found the experience of moving fast and light and picking what targets of opportunity I could quite liberating. If the SOE could improve my stealth and evasion skills, making me a better sniper, and point me at a few more important targets, then this unexpected opportunity could be beneficial to both of us.

'Glad to hear it.' Protheroe glanced over my shoulder, and nodded almost imperceptibly—out of the corner of my eye I saw a young man on crutches, his leg plastered, hovering by one of the closed doors leading off the main hall. 'Thank you, Conroy, I'll be right there.' He stood up and tucked the folded paper under his arm, returning his attention to me. 'We'll talk again once you're settled in. Hut four. But you'll probably want some breakfast first. I'm sure you can find the mess. Just follow your nose.' Then, without another word, he followed the hobbling man through the door he'd just emerged from, and disappeared.

FIVE

FOLLOWING MY NOSE did indeed take me to the mess hall, where I ate more than I'd expected to; the long journey to get here, my nighttime hike, and fitful sleep had sharpened my appetite more than I'd expected. At least I'd got rid of the suitcase: one of the huts I passed had a large number 4 painted on it, so I'd ventured inside, finding it deserted. It was clearly in use, though: three of the quartet of beds it contained were neatly made, with the lockers beside them supporting photographs and other personal possessions. The fourth had a bundle of blankets and pillows dumped on it, the locker open and empty, so I left my luggage on top of it and went to find something to eat.

The mess hall was reassuringly familiar, crowded and loud, although the number of women I could see scattered around the tables took a bit of getting used to. The food was surprisingly plentiful, too, after the rationing I'd experienced in London; I managed to snag a couple of rashers of bacon, two eggs, and a quite astonishing amount of some dark, rich flavoured wurst I didn't recognise, but which seemed surprisingly unpopular given how good it tasted.

'You're a brave man.' Charlie appeared at my shoulder and dropped into an adjacent seat, her own plate adorned with a kipper which she proceeded to dissect with undisguised relish. 'Not many people go for the haggis on their first day.'

'Or ever,' the young man with a pencil-thin moustache and Brilliantined hair on the other side of her put in. 'You do know what it's made from?'

'I'm sure you're going to tell me,' I said; so he did, looking faintly disappointed when I carried on eating with undiminished enthusiasm.

'It's all meat,' I said. 'And I grew up in Berlin. Believe me, the Germans'll put anything in a sausage.' I shrugged. 'Especially now, I guess.'

'Don't mind Jennings,' Charlie said. 'He's an idiot.'

Jennings nodded in cheerful agreement. 'Why else would I be here?' he asked.

'The scintillating company?' Charlie suggested, and he chortled appreciatively. I'd read about people chortling in Jeeves and Wooster stories, but I'd never expected to hear anyone do it in real life.

'Your sparkling repartee is the thing I'll miss the most,' he said, adding something in rapid French, which I didn't catch, but which made Charlie laugh. Then her expression became more serious.

'Do you know how soon you'll be leaving?'

Jennings shook his head. 'A few days, they tell me. Then it's croissants and caffe for breakfast, instead of sheep's offal. Sure I can't tempt you to join me?'

'I'll buy you a drink at the Deux Moulins when I get there. As soon as we've cleared Hitler's bully boys out of Paris.'

'I'll hold you to that.' He rose from the table, his plate empty—apart, I noticed, from a few scraps of stray haggis. 'Bonne chance, cherie.'

'And you.' She watched him go, a faint frown on her face, then returned her attention to the plate.

'Do you think he's ready?' I asked, and she turned the frown on me.

'Of course he is. Don't let the foppish façade fool you. Once he gets to France, Jerry won't know what's hit him.'

'Pleased to hear it,' I said, hoping she was right.

SIX

I RETURNED TO hut four feeling comfortably full, to be greeted by a full-throated chorus of 'Over There' the minute I opened the door. Two of the men singing I didn't recognise, although the third, his plastered leg propped up on the nearest bed, I remembered from my brief chat with Protheroe. Conroy: the man who'd interrupted us, and who, I assumed from what Charlie had said the night before, had found the walk up from the station a little more taxing than I had. The other two consisted of one short, dark-haired man, singing with gusto, and a taller fellow with red hair and a faintly embarrassed expression. The redhead was the first to step forward, a hand extended, which I took and shook.

'McMahon,' he said, with a faint Ulster accent. He indicated his two companions. 'That's Venables, and the crock in the corner's Conroy.'

'At least I'm alliterative,' Conroy said. He smiled, a

little uncertainly. 'Hope you didn't mind the serenade, but when Charlie told us you're a Yank, we couldn't resist it.'

'Half a Yank,' I said, 'and half Limey. But both appreciate the welcome.' I moved over to the bed I'd appropriated, moved my suitcase onto the floor and began to make it, folding the corners with West Point precision. 'I'm Fairburne, by the way.'

'So what do you do?' Venables asked. That was his way, I found: direct and to the point, with little time for small talk.

'I shoot people,' I said. 'I'm told I'm good at it.'

'Sniper. Good.' Conroy nodded. 'We can always use more of them. But I think the old man's got you in mind for infiltration. Set you up in Germany, co-ordinating resistance cells. There are still a few holding out against the Nazis, but there are damn few left, and they can do with all the help they can get.'

'I'd make a lousy spy,' I said. 'I'd stick out like a sore thumb.'

'We'll see.' Conroy didn't sound convinced. 'It's all about blending in, looking the part. You'd be surprised how easy it is when you get the hang of it.'

'That's your area of expertise, is it?' I asked, and he shook his head.

'Not really. I'm here to teach unarmed combat.' He grinned ruefully, and tapped the plaster cast. 'Obviously not an option at the moment, so the old man's got me pushing a pen instead. But I was an actor before the war.'

'Rather a good one, actually,' McMahon said. I must have looked surprised, because he added, 'I saw him in Oh, Kay! a few years ago.'

'Ah yes, Bolton rep. Happy days. Impecunious, but happy.' Conroy smiled reminiscently. 'Then I got called up. Found an unexpected talent for roughhousing, which came in handy in Norway. Which attracted the sort of attention that got me transferred here.'

'What did you do to catch their eye?' McMahon asked me, a little diffidently.

I shrugged. 'Potted a few Krauts on the retreat to Dunkirk.' The rest of it they didn't have to know. 'What about you?'

'Signals. I teach the trainees Morse code, how to set up and repair a radio in the field. And how to avoid being detected while they're doing it.' His brow furrowed. 'That's the trick, you've only got so long before the enemy triangulates your position. You have to send in short bursts, and keep moving if you can.'

'I'll bear that in mind,' I said. I glanced in Venables' direction. 'Care to share too?'

'Not much to tell,' he replied. 'I blow things up. Demolitions and sabotage. Build stuff, too, in theory, but there's not so much call for that around here.'

'He's being modest,' Conroy said. 'He's a dab hand at booby traps too. Left the Jerries a few surprises when we pulled out of Norway.'

'You were both there?' I asked.

Venables nodded. 'From beginning to end. I had it easy, but Conroy barely got out.'

I turned a questioning look on Conroy, who looked faintly embarrassed.

'These things get exaggerated,' he said. 'I got delayed a bit, that's all.'

'By the German army,' McMahon amplified. 'His patrol was ambushed, and he got left behind when they pulled back.'

'To be fair, they thought I was a goner,' Conroy said. 'Mortar shell brought down a wall, and they thought I was under it. I got hit by a flying brick, and when I came to, everyone was in the wrong uniform.'

'How did you get out?' I asked, intrigued.

'Luckily I had a scalp wound from being beaned; lot of blood, but no real damage. I pretended to be more out of it than I was, so they stuck me in a shed and sent for an officer who spoke English. He asked me a few questions, wrote me off as an imbecile, and took his pistol out to shoot me. So I took it off him, returned the favour, and legged it.'

'You took his gun off him?' I repeated, and Venables nodded.

'He's as good as he says he is at the rough stuff. And they thought he was only semi-conscious. So he caught them off-guard.'

'Basically, I was bloody lucky.' I found myself nodding in response. 'Come right down to it, and that's what really counts out there. It doesn't matter how good you are otherwise.'

'In my experience, being good helps too, though,' I said.

Conroy laughed. 'Doesn't it just?' he said.

SEVEN

THE NEXT COUPLE of days passed pleasantly enough, in a kaleidoscope of physical activity that I found almost restful after everything I'd been through in the past few months. In some ways it wasn't so different from West Point, but in others it took a good deal of getting used to, not least the lack of what I thought of as good military discipline. Protheroe hadn't been exaggerating about that in our first conversation— the SOE had its own way of doing things. We were there to learn how to operate alone, outside the chain of command, using our own initiative rather than following orders.

'You'll get used to it,' Protheroe assured me, after appearing unexpectedly on the rifle range the morning after my arrival. That was his way, I was to discover, roaming the camp, unobtrusively keeping an eye on things, stopping to exchange pleasantries with staff and trainees alike, before disappearing back into his office. He lowered a pair of binoculars, and nodded approvingly at the neat grouping of bullet holes in the centre ring of the thousand yard target. 'Getting used to your new toy, I see.'

'We're getting to know one another,' I agreed, rising from the prone position to talk to him more easily. The Lee Enfield was in most respects identical to the one I'd carried in France, but had been modified for sniping, and the difference in accuracy was phenomenal. The telescopic sight clearly showed targets so distant they'd have been all but completely hidden behind the foresight of a standard model, and the modified stock snuggled more securely in between my shoulder and cheek, damping the faint movements imparted by my breathing and heartbeat. With this, I could take a man cleanly with a single head shot from half a mile away, instead of just hoping to drop him with a lucky hit anywhere on the body, or simply send him scurrying for cover. 'I still need to get the feel of her at long range, but we're well on the way.'

'Her?' The major looked faintly amused. 'Should Charlie be feeling jealous?'

'Miss Barton?' I felt vaguely confused. 'Why should she be?'

'No reason.' Protheroe seated himself on one of the sandbags surrounding the firing position. 'But I'd like you to work together on stealth and evasion techniques. Chances are you'll both be spending a considerable amount of time behind enemy lines, and you could learn a lot from one another. You've had a lot of experience of striking from ambush and fading into the landscape, while what she doesn't know about blending into the civilian population you could write on the back of a postage stamp.'

'I'll give it a go,' I said, 'but I've already told you, I'm not interested in taking on the cloak and dagger stuff.'

'Duly noted.' He smiled quietly to himself, and got back to his feet. 'I'll see you back at the house.'

'Sir.' I nodded, still fighting the impulse to salute. Teaming up with Charlie seemed like a very bad idea to me, but orders were orders after all.

EIGHT

PREDICTABLY, CHARLIE WAS no more enthusiastic about the idea than I was.

'I haven't got time to be a babysitter,' she told me, frowning over a mug of tea in the mess hall. 'But he's usually right, so we might as well give it a go. Feel up for a night on the moors? Cross country, ten miles back to camp.'

'Whenever you do,' I told her, despite my reservations. Finding my way to the road from the railway station had been bad enough, and that had been with a clear path to follow. Striking out across open moorland, in the dark, would be a whole new ball game, but I was damned if I'd give her the satisfaction of crying off. 'Tonight?'

'Tomorrow,' she said. 'Things to do.' She drained the mug, which thudded onto the tabletop like audible impatience. 'Meet me at the orangery, nineteen hundred.'

'Will do.' I nodded. 'What's an orangery?'

Despite herself, she laughed. 'That big greenhouse thing behind the house. They were all the rage a hundred years ago if you had more money than sense.'

'I'm saving up for that,' I said. 'I've got about twelve cents to go.' To my surprise, she smiled at the feeble joke. Perhaps there was someone worth getting to know behind that brittle exterior after all.

'You're still ahead of the idiot who owns this pile.'

'Really?' Call me naive, but it hadn't really occurred to me that the house and estate belonged to someone. I'd just assumed that the War Office had acquired it somehow, and handed it over to the SOE.

'Oh yes. He's sitting out the war in an internment camp. One of Mosley's lot. Wanted to do a deal with Hitler, like Stalin did. Sign a non-aggression pact, and let them walk all over Europe.'

I snorted derisively. 'Like he wouldn't renege on it the moment it suited him.'

'Quite. But then fascists aren't particularly noted for their intelligence.'

'You don't have to tell me that,' I said. 'I've seen them in their native habitat.'

'Italy?' McMahon staggered up to the table and dumped a portable radio on it. The woodwork shook, almost spilling my coffee, and we all grimaced at the noise. 'Mussolini invented them, you know.'

'I did know,' I said, 'but I meant Germany. I grew up there.'

'Really?' McMahon looked at me curiously. 'You said you were a Yank. Half a Yank, anyway.'

'My dad's a diplomat. Got posted to the embassy in Berlin.'

'Ah. That's why Protheroe's got you earmarked for the German and Austrian Section. What there is of it.'

I sighed. 'Why's everyone so determined to turn me into a spy?'

'Because you'd be good at it?' Charlie suggested.

I shook my head. 'Trust me, I wouldn't. What you see is what you get.'

'Somehow I doubt that,' Charlie said, rising from her seat with an air of impatience, the lighter side of her I'd seen so recently tucked away out of sight again already. She didn't look back as she left.

Feeling faintly awkward, I turned to McMahon, and indicated the radio. 'What are you lugging that thing around for?'

His brow furrowed. 'There's something wrong with it. Damned if I can work out what it is, though.'

'It looks all right to me,' I said.

McMahon's expression of puzzlement increased. 'And me. But I was fiddling with it earlier, and knocked the tuner. Got a brief burst of static, which suddenly stopped. I thought one of the wires must be loose, but they're all firmly in place, and none of the tubes are going.'

'Could it have been interference?' I asked, memories

of listening to the BBC under the blankets as a child, on a cat's whisker radio Dad and I had built from a mail order kit, seeping their way to the surface. 'Plenty of electrical gadgets around here that could generate it. We had an icebox in our Berlin apartment that could...'

'Maybe,' McMahon said, sounding completely unconvinced. 'But it was on a very narrow frequency. That kind of interference usually swamps everything.'

'The icebox sure did,' I said. 'Whenever it cut in, the only music we could listen to was the pianola.' Something else occurred to me then, a brief memory flash of Charlie silhouetted against the dancing veil of the northern lights as I'd approached the road. 'The aurora's been pretty intense the last few nights. Could it have something to do with that?'

'Maybe.' Again, he didn't sound as though he believed that for a moment. 'But the same thing applies. And it wouldn't just cut off like that.' He sighed, and gave the radio the sort of glare my old drill instructor used to reserve for newly commissioned officers who thought their rank meant that they were in charge now. 'But I'll get to the bottom of it. One way or another.'

THE MESS HALL WAS quieter than usual when I entered it that evening, the buzz of conversation muted. As I

139

collected my food and headed for a table, I noticed several people staring at me, although I had no idea why. Perhaps I had spinach in my teeth, or the news that there was an American among them had been filtering out through the rumour mill.

Before I had any more time to think about it, a raised arm drew my attention to my hut mates, clustered together and talking intently among themselves. I returned the wave and headed towards them, finding a seat between Conroy, his crutches propped up against the table, and Venables, who lowered his hand as I approached.

'What's going on?' I asked, slicing the suet crust of my not-much-steak-and-even-less-kidney pudding, which promptly haemorrhaged gravy over the accompanying vegetables.

'You haven't heard?' Venables asked, sounding mildly surprised.

I shook my head. 'I've been on the firing range most of the day. The scope's taken a bit of work to zero in.' But the effort had been worth it. By the time the fading light and the growling of my stomach had driven me indoors I could have covered the group in the thousand yard target with a half crown, more or less, and hit a playing card at nearly a mile—providing I'd got the drop and the windage properly assessed. A good day's work, I felt, and I'd more than earned a hot meal. Then the sombre faces of my companions registered with me for the first time, and I began to realise that something was seriously wrong. 'What's going on?'

'Jennings is dead,' Venables said matter-of-factly, and returned his attention to his plate.

'What happened?' I asked. No point wasting breath on the usual expressions of bewilderment and denial. I'd seen too much action to be shocked or surprised by sudden death.

'The Germans were waiting for him,' Conroy said, shaking his head as though he couldn't really believe it. 'Right at the landing site. They shot him in his parachute harness on the way down.'

'He was dead before he even hit the ground,' Venables said. 'So we heard.'

'How's that possible?' I asked. 'How did they know he was coming?'

'That's what we'd all like to know,' McMahon said. 'The old man thinks there's a traitor in the resistance cell he was supposed to link up with, but of course they're denying it.'

'If they're still around to contact London, I'd be inclined to believe them,' I said. 'If there was a turncoat in the group, the Gestapo would have rolled up the whole network as soon as Jennings was confirmed dead.'

'Unless they're being used to feed us false information,' McMahon said.

'That's possible,' I conceded.

'It's the only explanation that makes any sense,' Conroy said. He glanced around the room, in an exaggeratedly conspiratorial manner. 'Unless you think there's a Nazi hiding under one of these tables with a wireless.'

'That's not funny.' Venables looked up from his plate, his eyes blazing. 'A good man just died. You can't make jokes about things like that.'

'No, you're right. Sorry.' Conroy looked appropriately abashed. 'Just trying to take it all in, I suppose.'

'We all are,' McMahon said, playing the peacemaker. He glanced across at me. 'He was popular around here. Everyone liked him.'

I remembered the way Jennings had bantered with Charlie over breakfast on my first day here, and nodded. 'I met him. Briefly. Seemed like one of the good guys.'

'Then I suppose that's why he died young,' Venables said, and began forking food into his mouth with the kind of unnecessary vigour the British display instead of expressing their feelings.

I WAS THE last of our group to leave the table. McMahon went first, muttering something about his faulty radio which I didn't quite catch, then Conroy rose a little awkwardly, grabbed his crutches, and hobbled away to report to Protheroe in the administration office.

'Looks like a long night,' he said as he went. 'London's going to want a full report on what went wrong. Don't wait up.'

'If they ever find out,' Venables said, staring after him. A few moments later he left too, and I found myself becoming restless. The muted atmosphere around me felt oppressive, and I needed some air.

It wasn't quite dark when I stepped outside, and I paused for a moment, inhaling the chill air gratefully. The sky was that soft silver colour I'd first noticed when I'd got off the train, and, despite the hour, I could see everything around me clearly. Hut four was only about a hundred yards away, but I needed a walk, so I turned in the opposite direction, intending to circle the garden surrounding the house and approach it from the other side.

Like a lot of country houses, the garden itself was divided into different sections by hedges and artful planting, and once I'd passed through the side gate in the thick stone wall surrounding it, it was easy to believe I was entirely alone, despite knowing that the bustle of the camp was continuing only a few yards away. I passed through a rose garden, in which a few stubborn blooms clung on despite the lateness of the year and the Scottish climate, before turning a corner into a secluded area surrounded by head-high hedging which, in happier times I'd been told, had been used for playing croquet.

And became aware that I was not alone.

I'd heard a few rustlings in the gloaming in the last few minutes, but thought little of it. The trees were home to a tribe of squirrels, who'd been energetically gathering provender for the oncoming winter, I'd heard the bark of foxes in the distance, although I'd yet to see one, and I could hardly have been the only person around here who'd felt like a stroll before bed. What I hadn't been prepared for was the sight of half a dozen men melting out of the shadows around me. Their faces were vaguely familiar from the mess hall, and none of them looked friendly. It was only when their leader stepped forward, his jaw set, and spoke, that I realised why.

'Enjoying your stroll, Mr Shafer?' So that was it. Somehow my old name had become known, and with it the inevitable prejudice. Even the old king had changed his family name to something less Germanic during the last war, and for much the same reason.

'It's Fairburne,' I said easily, relaxing my muscles so I could move fast if I had to. The odds weren't great if it came to a scrap, but I wouldn't be the worst off at the end of it. They were too confident, and too angry, both of which were fatal weaknesses in any kind of confrontation. I kept my tone calm and friendly while I looked for a weak spot. Their leader was tall and well muscled, but didn't hold his weight lightly, like a boxer would. A brute strength brawler, then. Easy to take down if I had to. That would give the rest something to think about, might even persuade the more sensible ones to back off. 'I haven't gone by Shafer since I was in diapers.'

'Not even in Germany?' Sceptical hostility oozed from his voice. 'Still got a few friends in Berlin, have you?'

'Sure,' I said. 'Himmler's invited me to his Bar Mitzvah.' A couple of the lurking shadows snickered quietly, and I could feel the simmering hostility begin to dissipate. But the group's leader seemed harder to convince.

'Joke all you want. But we're on to you.' He glared at me with naked hostility. 'I don't believe in coincidence.'

'Like someone whose father had a German name arriving just before an operation was blown, you mean?' I shrugged, with exaggerated scepticism. 'I mean, what are the odds?'

'Exactly.' The challenge was explicit now.

'That I'd find out about something planned and prepared for weeks in advance after only a few hours in camp, and get a message back to Germany before the evening was out?' Put like that, it was obvious how absurd the accusation had been. 'I'd be the best secret agent in history. With the world's fastest carrier pigeon.' This time the snickering was more widespread, and the ringleader bristled.

'I don't know how you did it. But I'll find out. Believe me.' His fists balled, and for a moment I thought I was going to have to deck him after all. 'Jennings was a friend of mine.'

'And mine,' a new voice cut in, and I turned to find Charlie standing at my shoulder. I hadn't heard her approach, and tried to keep my surprise off my face. Perhaps Protheroe did have a point—she was clearly very good at sneaking around. 'And you know perfectly well what he'd have to say about this kind of tomfoolery.'

'I was just saying, that's all.' The man's voice had become uncertain all of a sudden. 'It just seemed a bit suspicious.'

'Only if you're a complete idiot,' Charlie said. Then her voice softened. 'We all miss him. But turning on one another won't help anyone. Except Hitler.'

'No,' I said, 'it won't.' I looked the ringleader squarely in the eye, and, as I'd known he would, he blinked first. 'Jennings wasn't my friend, but I met him once, briefly, just after I got here. He made me feel welcome, and I liked him.'

The ringleader shifted his gaze to Charlie, who glared back. 'Now bugger off, before you make an even bigger fool of yourself.' She watched the group slink off into the darkness, and I saw the tension draining out of her. 'That could have been nasty.'

'Lucky you came along, then,' I said. I'd been joking, but she seemed to take the words at face value, and nodded thoughtfully.

'It's a bad business,' she said. 'Brings out the worst in people.'

'Wars tend to do that,' I said. 'But I'm sorry about your friend. Were you very close?'

She shook her head. 'Not in the way I suspect you're implying. He liked to flirt, but that was as far as he ever went. With women, anyway.'

'Ah,' I said, wondering if that had anything to do with the recent incident, and deciding it didn't matter anyway. Now we were alone together, I found I was running out of things to say. 'Would you like me to walk you back to your quarters?'

'How gallant.' Even in the fading light, I could make out her expression of amusement. 'But perhaps I'd better walk you back to yours. You seem to have something of a knack for finding trouble.'

'You don't know the half of it,' I agreed, falling into step beside her.

NINE

FROM THAT MOMENT on we were friends, whatever reservations she might have been harbouring about me vanishing as though they'd never existed. Ever since that evening she's been convinced she saved my hide, and I've never seen a reason to deny it, so I haven't. Even if I did, she wouldn't believe me; once Charlie makes up her mind about something, or someone, that's it. You might as well try to move Mount Rushmore with a teaspoon. But there was a connection between us now, and that made things a lot easier for me than it might otherwise have been. Her opinion mattered to a lot of people around the camp, and if Charlie Barton said you were on the level, then everyone else believed it too. Any lingering hostility towards me because of my old name vanished like the mist over the moorland.

'What are you looking so cheerful about?' Conroy greeted me as I returned to the hut. He was rummaging through his locker, and glanced up as I pushed open the door.

'Charlie Barton,' I said, without thinking. 'I ran into her just now. I think she's beginning to like me.'

'Oh.' Venables looked up too, from a gadget he was tinkering with, which had probably started out as an alarm clock, but which now looked as though it was intended to make a lot more noise when it went off than just ringing a bell. 'Better be careful with that one.'

Conroy nodded. 'If you don't believe him, ask the chap who tried to get a little too friendly during the film show last month. She broke two of his fingers.'

I smiled, in spite of myself. 'She sounds like the kind of girl my mom warned me about. I'd just about given up hope of getting to meet one.' I let the smile stretch. 'But don't worry, my intentions are honourable. I'm just happier it'll be easier to work together now.' I looked at Conroy curiously. 'What are you doing back here anyway? I thought you were needed in the office.'

'I am.' He fished something out of his locker and pocketed it. 'Left my lighter here. Just on the way back.' He hoisted himself up onto his crutches and stumped towards the door. As he passed McMahon he had to pivot on the spot to avoid the redheaded Irishman, who was kneeling on the floor, still engrossed in the bowels of his faulty radio set. 'Got enough room there?'

'Fine, thanks,' McMahon responded automatically,

barely registering the question at all, let alone the obvious sarcasm.

'Getting anywhere with it?' I asked, and he looked up at last, before nodding thoughtfully.

'I think so.' He seemed to register Conroy's presence for the first time, shuffling aside to make a little more room for him to pass. 'Something Conroy said gave me the idea.'

'Happy to be of service,' Conroy said flippantly, 'so long as there's no actual effort involved. What did I do?'

'Made that rather tasteless joke about a Nazi radio operator hiding in the mess hall,' McMahon said. 'It got me thinking.'

'Thinking what?' I asked, pretty sure I already knew.

'That perhaps what I'd picked up by accident wasn't just interference or a sparking wire. Maybe I got the last few seconds of a carrier wave, before someone switched off a transmitter nearby.'

I nodded. 'Makes sense. Why didn't you think of that first?'

'Because all the radio sets in camp were accounted for. And it was on a frequency none of them use. If it was a radio signal...'

'It wasn't from any of them,' I concluded, and McMahon nodded.

'So you're saying Conroy was right? There is a spy in the camp?' Venables looked worried.

Conroy frowned. 'It was just a stupid joke. But I'll talk to Major Protheroe as soon as I get back anyway. Can't be too careful.'

'If you think you should.' McMahon nodded. 'But it was probably just a stray transmission bouncing off the ionosphere. Like Fairburne said, the aurora's been very strong the last few nights. Now I've an idea of what to look for, I can keep listening out, try to narrow it down. I'm sure it's nothing important.'

TEN

'I'M NOT SO sure about that,' Charlie said, when I told her about the conversation the following day. 'If there was an enemy agent in the camp, they'd need a transmitter to report back. And the timing fits.'

'I see what you mean,' I said, stuffing a spare pair of socks into my rucksack. One lesson I'd learned very early on while dodging Nazi patrols in northern France was that warm dry feet made a disproportionate difference to your ability to stay alert. 'If what McMahon picked up really was the tail end of a transmission, it would have been at exactly the right time to alert the Germans to Jennings' arrival.'

'Exactly.' Charlie nodded. 'Which rather begs the question of who it could be.' Like me, she was wearing stout boots and standard battledress, her blonde hair tucked away under a black beret devoid of insignia; they were both slightly too large, the oversized hat hanging low over her eyes, the khaki uniform hanging loose around her, but somehow she managed to make the whole thing look incredibly stylish.

I shrugged, checking through the rest of the kit I'd collected. The air in the orangery was warm, and slightly sickly smelling, although the wrought iron and glass structure probably hadn't housed a citrus fruit in decades. Outside, though, the air was already growing chill, and the light beginning to fade. 'Could be anyone. There must be a couple of hundred people around here.'

'But not that many with access to operational information.' Her brow furrowed. 'We could probably narrow it down if we thought about it for a bit.'

'I'm sure Protheroe's got it all in hand,' I said, most of my attention on my mental inventory. Matches, ration bars, and a spare canteen, because another lesson I'd learned the hard way is that while there's always far too much water seeping into your boots, there's never quite enough of the drinkable stuff to keep you properly hydrated.

'I hope so.' Charlie looked over my shoulder and into the depths of my backpack, adopting an expression of exaggerated concern. 'Do you think you can manage without the kitchen sink?'

'I'll give it a try,' I said. 'But don't come crying to me when we need to wash the dishes.'

'I never cry. Punching people's a lot more effective.' But she was grinning again. 'Seriously, though, you think you're going to need all of this stuff?'

'I hope not,' I said, 'but I've done this for real. Being out in the field's not like an exercise. If you need something then and you haven't got it, you're really scr—ambling to catch up.' Charlie snickered, and I realised that of course she'd picked up on the hasty verbal swerve around inadvertently cussing in front of a lady. Which she was, undoubtedly, but by then I was thinking of her purely as a friend and a colleague.

'And you really think you'll be needing that?' She indicated the customised Lee Enfield I'd left leaning against a plant pot almost half as tall as I was.

'I need to get used to carrying it,' I said. A sniper's rifle is as much a part of them as their own right arm, and most of the ones I've met would no more have relinquished it than they would a body part. 'I suspect we've a long way to go together.' Which I was right about, of course, but how far, and for how long, I had no idea at all back then.

'If you say so,' Charlie said, picking up her own pack and shrugging it into place in a manner I pretended not to find extremely distracting. She bit her lower lip, thinking for a moment, then nodded decisively. 'I'd better take the Thompson, then. Protheroe said we're supposed to be learning from each other after all.'

'You'll thank me later,' I said, thinking of her sneaking into position for an ambush somewhere in occupied France—but as it turned out, we'd both be grateful for the decision a lot sooner than that.

Before leaving the oversized greenhouse we checked the route Charlie had planned for our cross-country hike on a map she pulled from a pocket of her battledress. I nodded approval. Too many rookies would simply have stuck it in their backpack, where it would have remained relatively inaccessible.

'We're heading out through the main gate, then skirting the sides of the valley here,' she said, tracing the route with her finger. 'Down to the shores of the loch. Then circle back this way to the camp. Home in time for breakfast.'

'I hope so,' I said, thinking about the rough terrain, and the ankle-snagging heather. Conroy had managed to break his leg on the path up from the station, and that had been easy going compared to the hike we were about to undertake. I lifted the Lee Enfield and slid the shoulder strap into place. A comforting sense of familiarity came with it, and for some reason my confidence rose. A little of what I was feeling must have shown on my face, because Charlie was grinning at me as she tucked the map away again.

'Boys and their toys,' she said.

'And girls,' I reminded her. 'We still need to pick up your spray and pray before we go.'

'I don't need to pray. I've got my marksman rating, thank you very much. What I shoot at, I hit.'

'Really?' I raised an eyebrow. 'Where I come from, that's fighting talk.'

'Fine. Ten bob says you miss a target before I do.' She stared a challenge at me. 'Firing range tomorrow afternoon?'

'You're on,' I said. 'But pistols, so we start out even. I'd have too big an advantage with this.'

'Better and better,' she said, and grinned at me again. 'So it's true what they say about a fool and his money.'

'Who's got yours, then?' I asked, and she laughed.

'Me, and I'm keeping it.' She led the way out into the open air, which seemed cold and fresh after the clammy atmosphere of the orangery. 'This way.'

A short detour took us to her hut, and I waited outside while she went in to fetch the submachine gun. I shivered a little, and blew on my hands, grateful for the extra layers of clothing I'd donned. I'd warm up a lot slogging through the heather, no doubt, but right now it was cold and getting colder.

Hurrying footsteps grabbed my attention, and I turned to see McMahon running towards the house.

'What's up?' I asked, as he approached.

'I need to see Protheroe,' he panted, barely slowing down. 'Picked up a new transmission. Somewhere close!'

Then he was gone. A door banged closed behind me, and Charlie appeared at my shoulder, staring after McMahon.

'What's up with him?' she asked.

ELEVEN

WE HESITATED FOR a moment after I'd told her, debating whether or not to postpone our exercise, but quickly agreed there was no point. If there was a traitor with a hidden radio somewhere in the camp we were still no closer to finding out who it was, and there could be an innocent explanation for whatever McMahon had picked up. So we started for the main gate, striding out along the long, curving drive I remembered from the night of our arrival.

I noticed it first. As we got closer to Lennox's cottage, a thin sliver of yellow light became visible, standing out in the gathering darkness. The aurora wasn't painting the sky this evening, but the moon and the stars were bright, bathing everything in a soft, blue-grey luminescence in which we could both see clearly once our eyes had adjusted. 'Something's not right,' I said.

'No,' Charlie agreed. 'He's never that careless about the blackout.'

By mutual unspoken agreement we slowed our pace, moving to the edges of the drive, where the shadows of the hedge afforded us some cover. Protheroe had been right that Charlie had a real flair for this sort of thing; she moved as quietly as I did, testing every footfall before placing her full weight on the ground. The softest of scraping sounds accompanied our progress, our boots sliding across the grass fringing the gravelled driveway, nudging the occasional twig out of the way before it could betray our presence with an audible snap.

We reached the fence surrounding Lennox's vegetable patch, and looked the cottage over carefully. Nothing moved, and no sounds came from inside. We waited. Nothing continued to happen. The wrought iron gates beside it cast tangled shadows across the ground.

'Cover me,' we both said at the same time. 'I'm going in.' We looked at one another; despite the absurdity of the moment, neither of us felt like laughing.

'Stay here,' Charlie said, unslinging the Thompson, and glancing pointedly at my Lee Enfield. 'You're the long-range specialist, so you should be the one to stay on overwatch.'

'Fair point,' I agreed, readying the rifle. I went down on one knee next to the hedge, where the shadows were thickest, and raised the long arm, squinting through the telescopic sight. 'The door's ajar.' I could see it clearly, magnified in the centre of the scope. 'That's where the light's coming from.'

'Then that's my way in.' Charlie snapped the safety catch off, and tapped the magazine, making sure it was properly inserted. She had a second box taped to the one in the breech, upside down, so she could reload in a hurry simply by ejecting it and turning it round—a popular modification with shooters familiar with the Thompson and its idiosyncrasies. Even firing short bursts, it could burn through the twenty rounds a standard magazine held uncomfortably fast, and no one likes fumbling for reloads in the middle of a firefight. The ones you see in the movies usually have the fifty round drum magazines, but Charlie didn't like them; they were prone to jamming, took longer to change, and you needed to pull the bolt back to do it, which took precious additional seconds. Seconds you might not have if your target was returning fire, and had a good eye. 'Watch my back.'

'You can count on it,' I said, reflecting that our exercise had suddenly got a lot more serious. For all I knew Lennox had simply gone out for some air and fumbled the latch, but I didn't really buy that; all my instincts were telling me that something was seriously wrong, and Charlie clearly felt the same way. She approached the small house at a crouching run, keeping low and to the shadows, flattening herself against the wall as soon as she reached it.

I swept the scope from side to side, failing to find anyone lurking in ambush, then raised it to check the windows. All were tightly shuttered, only the most tenuous illumination leaking from around them. I returned my attention to the door, covering it, alert for any sign of movement, but, again, there was nothing. I raised a hand, signalling that all was clear.

Charlie acknowledged that with a wave of her own, and crept along the side of the cottage, still keeping low to pass under the sill of an intervening window. Reaching the door, she rose to her full height, and lifted the Thompson to a vertical position, ready to level it the instant she was inside. This was the moment of truth. Then, to my surprise, instead of kicking the door open and levelling the submachine gun to cover her entrance, she sank down on her haunches, running a hand around the door frame as she descended. Satisfied that there were no booby traps she rose to her feet again, took two deep breaths, then moved almost too fast for me to follow through the scope.

Pivoting round the edge of the doorway she kicked the panel open, and disappeared inside, silhouetted for a moment against the glare of the yellow rectangle. My eyes now used to the soft natural glow of the evening, I squinted, momentarily dazzled by the harsh electric light. I could see very little inside, apart from the corner of an armchair and part of a framed landscape set against some bland floral wallpaper.

Shadows flickered across my narrow view of the room, Charlie moving around, presumably. I strained my ears, but heard nothing apart from the hooting of an owl somewhere across the glen.

No shouting or shooting meant that she was all right, but intensified my sense of foreboding. If Lennox hadn't reacted to the sudden appearance of a young woman brandishing a tommy gun in his living room, something was definitely wrong.

'Karl!' Charlie appeared in the doorway again, gesticulating in my direction. 'Get in here!'

I was up and moving in an instant, keeping the rifle ready for use. Just because the danger wasn't obvious, that didn't mean it didn't exist.

'What's the matter?' I just had time to ask, before my eyes answered the question for her. Lennox was at home after all—but very dead, slumped in the armchair facing the one I'd seen through the door. A shotgun was propped between his knees, and most of his chest was missing. From the way the blood and viscera had spread, he'd obviously been sitting there when the gun went off. 'Oh.'

'Oh indeed.' Charlie was looking around the room with an air of curiosity that was either a sign of analytical detachment or shock, although by now I would have put my money on the former.

'Suicide, do you think?' I asked.

Charlie nodded. 'Looks that way. It didn't discharge

accidentally while he was cleaning it. The patches are still in the dresser drawer, along with his gun oil.'

I frowned. Something about the scene didn't look right, although I couldn't quite put my finger on what it was. 'But why, though? Did you find a note?'

Charlie shook her head. 'They don't always leave one, you know.' She put her gun down, leaning it slightly incongruously against an empty umbrella stand, and I thought about doing the same, but decided against it. I had an uncomfortable feeling that things weren't adding up, and I wasn't about to relinquish my own weapon until I understood what had happened here. After a moment I compromised, slinging it across my back again.

'We need to report this,' I said. 'Get someone who knows what they're doing over here.'

'Already done.' Charlie indicated a telephone on the corner of the dresser. 'I called Protheroe. He's on his way with a brace of MPs.'

'Good,' I said. Perhaps a trained eye could make more sense of this than I could. Despite myself I walked around the corpse, looking for anything that might help. As I shifted my head, a faint gleam of reflected light in the middle of Lennox's jacket lapel caught my attention. I bent closer to get a better view, trying to ignore the immediately adjacent sights and smells. 'Look at this.'

'Seen one dead gamekeeper, seen them all,' Charlie

said, coming over anyway, and narrowing her eyes. 'What have you found?'

'There's something on his lapel,' I said. 'Looks like metal.' A thin silver sliver, no more than an eighth of an inch long, shining against the fabric. 'What do you think that is?'

Charlie snorted. 'You don't spend much time around women, do you? It's a brooch pin.' She turned the lapel over, revealing the back. Something was pinned there all right, but it wasn't a brooch. She said something extremely unladylike.

'It's a badge,' I said, unnecessarily. 'And I'm guessing it's not a good one.' A white lightning bolt zigzagging across a dark blue circle, surrounded by a white border.

'You guess right. It's a bad badge,' Charlie confirmed. 'British Union of Fascists. Mosley's lot.' From her expression I half-expected her to spit at the corpse, but she didn't. 'Hitler sympathisers to a man. And woman, unfortunately.'

'Makes sense, I suppose,' I said. 'If the owner of the estate's a fascist, then his employees might have similar sentiments.'

'You'd think,' Charlie said. 'But Lennox was thoroughly checked out. He wouldn't have been allowed to work here if there had been the slightest doubt about his loyalties.'

'Then he can't have been checked thoroughly

enough,' Protheroe said, appearing at the door, a couple of red caps in tow. He must have overheard the end of our conversation, because he made a beeline for the corpse, scowling at the incriminating badge in the same way Charlie had. 'What else have you found?'

'Nothing much,' I said. I glanced at Charlie. 'We were about to make a more thorough search when you arrived.'

'We were.' She nodded confirmation. 'There must be some evidence around here that'll help make sense of this.'

'Something like this, you mean?' I'd opened a drawer at random, and found a thin booklet full of numbers. Protheroe's scowl intensified.

'Exactly like that,' he said. 'A cipher key. It looks as though we've found our mysterious radio operator.'

'But not his radio,' I said.

Protheroe shook his head. 'Not yet,' he said. 'But we will.' He turned to the red caps. 'Tear this place apart. If it's here we'll find it.' He turned back to me, his expression shrewd. 'Something on your mind, Fairburne?'

'I'm not sure,' I admitted. 'Something about this whole setup seems... I don't know, just wrong, somehow.'

'Same here,' Charlie put in unexpectedly. 'If Lennox was a traitor, why advertise it by wearing a badge?

Even a hidden one? It's the sort of thing villains in movie serials do.'

'Overconfidence, perhaps,' Protheroe said. 'People like that can get a thrill out of feeling superior to the people they're fooling. It's quite common in espionage.'

'You'd know more about that sort of thing than I would,' I said. I was beginning to feel surplus to requirements now the military police were here, and Protheroe had taken charge. 'Do you still need us?'

'I don't think so, no,' Protheroe said. 'You might as well carry on with your night exercise. Conway can debrief you in the morning. We're liable to be here for some time.' A loud crash from upstairs underlined the point. 'With any luck, by tomorrow morning we'll know exactly what we're dealing with.'

Which was quite true, as things turned out. Unfortunately, by that time, it was far too late.

TWELVE

HALF AN HOUR later we might as well have been on the moon for all the signs of human habitation we could see, but we were still talking about what we'd found, instead of concentrating on what we were doing. Which wasn't particularly wise, the going underfoot just as treacherous as I'd anticipated, but once you've discovered something like that, it tends to stick in the mind.

'It doesn't make sense,' I said, for about the dozenth time. 'If Lennox was a spy, how could he have found out about Jennings' mission? He never goes near the house.'

Charlie shrugged, a shifting shadow in the moonlight. 'He was around the estate all the time, and he was used to sneaking up on game. No telling what he might have overheard. Particularly if he was hiding somewhere.'

'It's possible,' I conceded. 'But there was something about the body. It didn't look right.'

'Both barrels through the ribcage can do that,' Charlie said.

I nodded, forgetting she couldn't see the movement. 'That's just it. Most suicides by shotgun put the barrel under the chin. That way they can reach the trigger with a thumb, and...' I broke off, as realisation suddenly dawned.

'Perhaps he didn't want to spoil his good looks,' Charlie said, stopping to scan the horizon with a pair of binoculars. 'Good. I can see the loch already. We're making excellent time.'

'How could he have reached the trigger from that position?' I asked, the thought I'd just had hardening suddenly into certainty. 'He would have had to lean right over the barrels. The blast would have taken him in the stomach, not the ribs. And he would have collapsed on the floor, not back into the chair.'

'You've been reading too much Agatha Christie,' Charlie said, but she lowered the binoculars anyway, and turned to face me.

'Not so much,' I said, 'but I've seen a lot of dead guys. And Lennox looked dead wrong.'

'So you're saying the scene was staged,' Charlie said. She still sounded sceptical, but at least she was considering it. 'How, and by who?'

'How's easy enough,' I said. 'Our murderer just walks in. Maybe he waits for Lennox to get back from his rounds. Gamekeepers always carry a gun with them, right?'

'Right,' Charlie agreed.

'So Lennox comes home, puts the gun down wherever he usually stashes it, and the bad guy comes in behind him and grabs it. Or perhaps they already knew where it was kept.'

'That wasn't a secret,' Charlie said. 'He always put it in the umbrella stand by the door. Where he could get at it in a hurry. Anyone entering or leaving by the main gate while the door was open could have seen it.'

I nodded, the picture in my head becoming clearer. 'So maybe the murderer didn't have to wait for him. They could have walked straight into the house and grabbed it then and there.'

Charlie nodded, too, following my train of thought. 'He didn't even have time to get out of the chair. Took both barrels at point-blank range.' An edge of anger seeped into her voice. 'Poor sod. He probably didn't even realise what was happening until it was too late.'

'Right,' I agreed, the rest of the pieces falling into place. 'Then the killer planted the badge and the codebook, and skedaddled. They must have known it was only a matter of time before the body was discovered.'

'Giving them time to dispose of the radio,' Charlie concluded.

'Or use it,' I said thoughtfully, remembering

McMahon running past her hut while I'd been waiting outside. 'The timing doesn't make sense otherwise. We found Lennox just after McMahon picked up another transmission.'

'So he was killed first, then the murderer sent another message.' A tinge of doubt came into her voice. 'But why would they do that? There aren't any operations planned for tonight.'

'None that we know about,' I said. 'That's not the same thing.'

'We need to talk to Protheroe,' Charlie said decisively. 'If you're right, the traitor's still on the loose, and there are other lives at stake. Our little ramble will have to wait.'

'So what's our quickest route back?' I asked. 'The way we came?'

'No.' Charlie turned and pointed. 'If we cut back that way we'll reach a path running from the camp down to the sea loch. It's rough, but a lot faster.'

'Then let's go.' I raised the rifle, and peered though the telescopic sight, sweeping it across the heather. If she said the path was there it undoubtedly was, but I couldn't see any sign of it in the moonlight. I turned towards the distant glint of sea water, hoping to pick up the beach end of the track and trace it back, but again I was disappointed. I was about to lower the weapon, when I caught sight of something else: a dark shape against the rippling silver, a few hundred yards from the shoreline. 'Can you see that? There's something in the water.'

'What kind of something?' Charlie raised her binoculars, and adjusted the focus. 'Oh my God. Tell me that's not what I think it is.'

'That depends,' I said. 'If you think it's a whale, you're wrong. But if you think it's a U-boat...'

'We're all in very big trouble,' she finished.

THIRTEEN

WE MADE AS much speed as we could down the slope towards the path, but I knew with sickening certainty that we wouldn't be fast enough. The heather snagged at our boots with every step, threatening to pitch us over, and after a few moments I called a halt.

'This is crazy,' I said. 'If we keep this up one of us'll break a leg like Conroy did.'

'He didn't break it here,' Charlie said, slightly breathless from our exertions. 'It was in plaster when he arrived. He got caught in an air raid the night before he left London.'

'That was bad luck,' I said.

'Depends on how you look at it.' She joined me behind the cover of a large boulder, slick with mosses and lichens. 'There are plenty of blitzed Londoners who'd be grateful to have got away with just a fracture.' She raised the binoculars again. 'Merde.' I lifted the Lee Enfield and peered through the scope, centring it on the dark shadow rising from the water. A flicker of movement drew my attention to the edge of the image, and I shifted the centre of the sight to follow it. 'We're out of time.'

'Looks that way,' I agreed. A couple of inflatable boats were halfway between the shingle beach and the looming bulk of the submarine. Dark figures were plying paddles, while others kept watch. It was hard to tell how many men were in each dinghy, but my best guess was between four and six. 'That's definitely a landing party.'

'Which explains the last transmission,' Charlie said. 'Either our traitor was giving them the all clear, or they were telling him to keep his head down.'

'Probably both,' I said, going prone, the heather prickly even through the weave of my battledress. I pressed the stock of the rifle into my cheek. 'I'll buy you as much time as I can. Get back to the camp and warn them there's an attack on the way.'

'Just like that?' Her voice was incredulous. 'You really think you can hold them off on your own?'

'Unless you've got a better idea,' I said.

'Not really.' She shook her head. 'I don't suppose you've got a flare pistol in that overstuffed bag of yours?'

''Fraid not,' I told her. 'See what I mean about scrambling now?'

'Absolutely.' There was a faint rustle of movement,

and then she was gone, with a final 'good luck.' Which I was going to need in spades.

I stilled my breath, slowing my heartbeat, moving the scope to cover the nearest of the inflatables. It still seemed tiny this far away, even magnified, looking little larger than my thumbnail in the centre of the sight. But I'd hit far smaller targets on the shooting range at about the same distance. I had a cartridge in the breech already, from our cautious approach to Lennox's cottage, so I eased the safety off with the pad of my thumb. The dinghy bobbed up and down on the waves, adding its own oscillation to the gentle motion of the scope imparted by my breathing and the rhythmic thudding of my heart. Too experienced to snatch at the shot I waited, letting the pattern establish itself, not thinking about it, feeling my way into the moment.

I pulled the trigger without conscious thought, hearing the bark of the rifle, and feeling the stock kick back against my shoulder, riding the recoil by reflex. I worked the bolt, ejecting the spent cartridge and inserting another, then returned my eye to the scope. I hadn't hit anything, but the shot had clearly gone close enough to be noticed; the men plying the paddles had redoubled their efforts, and the dark silhouettes had sunk as low as they could, as if the flimsy fabric gunwales could have afforded any protection at all against a bullet.

A sudden flash of memory overwhelmed me for a moment, of crouching as low as I could in an overloaded boat while bullets churned the water, reaching out to the nearest of the frantic swimmers around me while the waves turned red, hauling him half aboard before realising he was already dead and then pitching him back to make room for another survivor.

Then I forced the thought away. These men were invaders intent on slaughter, not people I could afford to feel any sympathy for. I was all that stood between them and the massacre of my oblivious comrades. But a small part of me stayed in that small, bobbing refuge, all too aware of what they'd be feeling.

I took a deep breath, and let it go, allowing my reflexes to take over again. There was no hurry, they were still over a hundred yards from the shore. Don't think, just feel, the rifle an extension of my own body, the small inflatable drifting gently through the centre of the scope. Feel the wind against my face, fluctuating gently, and move the muzzle a fraction to compensate. Raise the sight to allow for the difference in altitude between the hillside and the gently bobbing boat on the waves so far below, and the fall of the bullet as its momentum dissipates. Hear the crack and feel the recoil as the gun discharges itself.

This time one of the indistinct figures pitched backwards, raising a faint spray of silver droplets as it hit the water, dead or alive, there was no way to tell at this distance. But the men wielding the paddles were back watering frantically, reaching out to haul him in. Perfect. I'd got the range now, and chambered another round without even thinking about it.

The next shot went low, and for a moment I thought I'd flubbed it: but the frantic activity in the distant inflatable redoubled, and it seemed to be riding a little lower in the water. I'd holed it, and it was losing air fast. Not quite fast enough for my liking, though, so I fired again. Another of the men pitched over the side, but whether I'd hit him or he was simply jumping for it to avoid getting tangled up in the rapidly deflating dinghy I couldn't tell. Didn't care either, if I'm honest. By now that group of Brandenburgers were long past being an immediate threat, so I turned my attention to the second inflatable.

'Verdammt!' I snarled, reverting to German, as I still do when swearing in English doesn't seem powerful enough—being able to add the intensifier makes a surprising amount of difference when I've strong feelings to relieve. The other boat had beached while I was concentrating on the first one, running in behind a small headland which shielded both it and its occupants from view. I'd have to move to get a line of sight on them; something I was inclined to do anyway, as anyone watching from the conning tower of the submarine could have spotted the muzzle flashes of the Lee Enfield. Not that there was much they could do about it from that distance, but if the landing party had a portable radio with them they could be warned of my presence.

No sooner had the thought occurred to me than a signal lamp began flashing, a rapid stream of Morse code. In plain German, thank goodness; either they hadn't got time to code it, or they'd been rattled by this sudden setback. Unexpected resistance. Team two under fire. Proceed with caut…

Enough of that, I thought, cutting the message off halfway with a single bullet. The bright, flickering light had made an obvious target, even at that range; again, I couldn't tell if I'd smashed it with a lucky shot, disabled the signaller, or simply sent him ducking for cover, but it was all the same to me. Time to move. At least it seemed the intruders were without voice communication, which was something.

I ran in the direction Charlie had taken, hoping to find the path she'd mentioned. It was dollars to doughnuts that the Brandenburgers would be taking it, moving as fast as they could to their objective in the hope of launching their attack before anyone in the camp became aware of their presence. I swore again as the heather snagged at my boots, almost pitching me over, and recovered my balance in the nick of time. If I kept this up I'd break my neck, never mind a leg.

That's when I saw it, a faint dark line winding through the scrub, about fifty yards in front of me. The path, at last. There was no sign of Charlie, even when I looked through the scope in the direction of the camp; she must be halfway back there by now. Good. Help was on the way. I just had to hold the raiding party until it arrived.

Which was going to be easier said than done. I looked around for a suitable ambuscade. Several outcrops like the one I'd used before were protruding from the ground cover, and I assessed them critically. The nearest offered a good vantage point, but was steep sided and slippery with overgrowth—it would be an effort to scramble up, and I'd be an easy target getting down if I had to move position in a hurry. Which I would, I'd only get a couple of shots off before the raiders spotted my position, and I became a fire magnet. The first rule of successful sniping is shoot and run, before the enemy has a chance to retaliate.

The next furthest position sloped gently, offering a good firing platform overlooking the trail, so I made for that, finding it almost perfect. The lip would offer me a reasonable amount of concealment and hard cover against return fire, and I could easily move away from it under the refuge of a few straggling gorse bushes. A couple of boulders stood nearby, which I could make for when I had to change position, and after that I'd just have to make it up as I went along.

I listened intently, hearing nothing but the wind in the scrub, but that didn't mean the enemy weren't already close; after the warning they'd received they'd want to reach their objective as quickly as possible. There was no point in hesitating, so I headed for the rock I'd picked out as quickly as I dared.

The vantage point was perfect, and I set up as fast as I could without hurrying. Haste is the sniper's worst enemy, sending shots wild and betraying their position. I lay prone on the hard, cold stone, feeling mosses and lichens smearing my clothes, and secured the gun into my shoulder. As comfortable as I could be under the circumstances, I slowed my breathing, focusing the scope on the narrow, winding track, which reminded me of the one I'd struggled up from the station. I hoped the comparison was apt; if it was, the Brandenburgers would be moving relatively slowly, allowing me a couple of easy kills before they could retaliate.

I swept the scope along the length of it, back down towards the beach, seeing no sign of movement other than a rabbit or two rustling through the heather. Or maybe they were grouse. Either way they weren't likely to be carrying guns, so I could safely ignore them. The trail curved out of sight, behind a craggy outcrop, so I centred the scope on that, and waited.

Silence descended, in which the loudest sound I could hear was my own breathing, and the slow, measured thudding of my heart. Overlaid with those were the susurration of the wind, the rustling of the heather, and, somewhere so distant I wasn't sure if I was actually imagining it, the rhythmical hiss of the waves lapping against the shingle of the beach.

Then another sound, so faint I had to strain my ears to catch it. The whisper of footfalls among the undergrowth, and a hastily suppressed cough. The raiders were coming.

FOURTEEN

FOREWARNED, I KEPT the scope on the bend in the trail by the rock, waiting for the first man to appear. After a moment a shadow elongated, as a human figure emerged from behind it. I let my finger rest lightly on the trigger, a round already chambered, and waited. He was moving as fast as caution allowed, at a little more than walking pace, a submachine gun held ready for instant use.

I held my fire; there was no point in revealing my presence until I was sure of all of them.

A few seconds later another man appeared, and then a third, maintaining a constant distance between one another; after a moment I realised it was just enough to make it harder for someone like me lurking in ambush to target more than one of them at a time. It also made it easy for me to count them off, and when a few more seconds had passed after the emergence of the sixth member of the squad, I could be reasonably certain that there were no more to come.

I considered my options. Taking the point man out first would alert them all. Taking the last would give me a precious few seconds to reload, and possibly drop another before any of the survivors realised what was happening and began to retaliate, by which time I intended to be somewhere else entirely. On the other hand, the squad leader would probably be one of the men in the middle, and if I could identify him and take him out the whole unit would be thrown into confusion. Or would it? These were highly trained commandos, used to thinking for themselves, and would probably shrug off the setback. Besides, it would open up a gap in the line, restricting my options for a follow-up target.

The last man it was, then. I centred the scope, then shifted it a fraction, instinctively allowing for the breeze I could feel against my right cheek, the left warm against the wood of the stock. My finger tightened on the trigger. I could already sense the path the bullet would take, from the muzzle of the Lee Enfield to the bridge of his nose and on out through the back of his head. Then, at the last minute, I checked the motion. A metallic glint had flashed, just for a fraction of a second, on his torso, moonlight ricocheting from something hanging from his webbing.

Distracted, I shifted the scope, and spotted what I'd almost missed. He had a bandolier of grenades slung across his chest. I pictured the havoc they would wreak if he reached the camp with them; a single one thrown into a Nissen hut would kill everyone inside it. If I'd had any doubt at all about their mission, it was dissipated in that instant. Create as much carnage as possible, and seize what intelligence they could before withdrawing. SOE agents all across occupied Europe would be blown, and their resistance networks along with them. Whether their spy would go with the raiders, or be left behind posing as a lucky survivor to continue their treachery, I couldn't tell, but it was a moot point right now anyway.

I retargeted, aiming for the fellow's torso. It would be a much trickier shot than the one I'd intended, but with any luck it would give me an edge, and even if it didn't have the effect I was hoping for, the bullet would still drop him. I stilled my breathing again, aiming for a far smaller target than the head shot I'd originally intended. Breath, wind, heartbeat, gravity and target performed their intricate dance, and intuition pulled the trigger before I'd even realised I'd done it.

The effect was all I'd hoped for, and more, the bullet striking one of the grenades and detonating it. The man disappeared in a mist of blood and viscera, the scything shrapnel ripping the next man in line apart as the blast wave spread. The others threw themselves flat in the heather, and stared around in shock, trying to work out what had just happened and who was responsible.

Before they had the chance, I ejected the cartridge and chambered another round. Two down, and four to go. The odds still weren't great, but I was tilting them in my favour.

I swung the scope, searching for a target, but they were too well trained or experienced to make any rookie mistakes, like standing up to look around, or, better still, making a run for it so I could shoot them in the back. The heather rippled, as they began to crawl through it, and I focused on the nearest patch of disturbed vegetation, hoping to get a clear sight of a potential target.

'Who's down?' a voice asked, in German, pitched low so as not to carry. The squad leader, without a doubt, although which of the rustling heather patches he was I couldn't tell.

'Helmut and Dieter,' a second voice replied. 'They were right behind me.'

'So what the hell happened?' a third cut in, and I had an idea. It was bold, and probably stupid, but I wasn't going to get another target unless I did something that fell into at least one of those categories.

'Minefield!' I called in the same language. 'There's a sign over here!' As I'd hoped, the boulders I'd taken refuge among wrapped my voice in overlapping echoes, obscuring my exact whereabouts.

The leader swore. 'Great. Something else they didn't bother to brief us about.' One of the shadows in the darkness began to rise, taking on human form. 'Move carefully, test every—'

I fired instinctively, barely bothering to aim, knowing even as I did so that the shot was a good one. It took him in the throat as he stood up, severing his spinal column on the way out; he must have been dead before he hit the ground. And even before he did I was moving, ducking back behind the lip of the boulder, scrambling down and ready to make a run for the shelter of the gorse bushes.

Only to dive back behind the sheltering stone as a blizzard of submachine gun fire spanged from the rock, throwing sharp-edged splinters into my face. At least one of the raiders must have spotted the muzzle flash of my last shot, and was retaliating. Not that he had much chance of hitting me, at least while I had a couple of tons of boulder to hide behind, but he was keeping me pinned real good.

'What the hell?' one of his compatriots asked.

'The British sniper. He's up there.' The firing had stopped. 'Behind that rock. You and Kurt circle round that way, and I'll take him from this side. He's got nowhere to go.'

I wormed my way across to the other side of the rock, to see two shadowy figures, keeping low, scuttling up the hill towards me. I fed another round into the Lee Enfield, and went prone again, raising the sight. But they knew what they were doing. Before

I could even draw a bead on the nearest, one of them had raised his submachine gun, and sent a burst in my direction which sent me squirming back behind the boulder. I rolled, risking a look out of the other side of my rocky refuge, only to see the third man halfway up the slope, circling wide to get a clear shot. I raised the rifle, and cracked off a snap shot just as he made it to the cover of the bushes I'd been counting on to conceal my retreat. The bullet went wide, but he kept his head down; I knew it wouldn't hold him off for long and I was right. Even as I worked the bolt, another burst of automatic fire whined over my head.

I considered my options. I could wait for this guy to make his move and hope I could take him out, or face the other two. Their submachine guns weren't accurate at this range, but their rate of fire was high enough to be a threat anyway—I'd be just as dead from a lucky hit as a well-aimed one.

I rolled back to the other side of the giant stone, and raised the scope, but I had no real need of it to see where the two raiders were now—close enough to see me, and open up again the minute I revealed my presence. I ducked back, bullets whining around my head, ricocheting from the stone again, the petrified shrapnel stinging the back of my hands. I blinked my eyes clear of pulverised rock. Worse still, they'd spread out; even if I could get a clear shot at one of them, I'd never have time to reload and shift my aim before the other returned the favour. And in the meantime, the other guy was getting ready to shoot me in the back.

At least I could reduce the odds a little further, though. I peered cautiously round the boulder again, getting ready to shoot on the fly and hope for the best. But before I could pick a target another figure rose from the heather behind the two raiders, aiming a submachine gun of its own.

The first burst of the Thompson took the left-hand Nazi clean in the back, pitching him forward onto the springy undergrowth, practically ripped in half by the hail of bullets. The other took a moment to react, presumably having taken the sound for another attack on me, but as he turned to face Charlie I fired, dropping him instantly.

'What the hell—' I started to yell.

'Stay down!' She fired once more, the burst hissing over my head. I turned to see the last man collapsing, his chest a bloody ruin, the gun he'd been aiming at me falling to the ground. I stood slowly.

'What are you doing here?' I tried again.

'Saving your arse, by the look of it.' The words were jaunty, but her expression was anything but. First kills will do that to you.

'You were supposed to go warn the camp.' I tried to sound hacked off about it, but couldn't manage any tone other than grateful.

Charlie shrugged. 'I'd never have got there in time.

So I hid, and watched your back.'

'Protheroe said you were good at the sneaky stuff,' I said.

'I am.' This time she definitely sounded smug. 'And speaking of Protheroe, we need to have a word with him as soon as possible. I've worked out who the traitor is.'

'Me too,' I said.

FIFTEEN

'THE TRAITOR WAS Lennox,' Protheroe said, leading us into his office, and dropping the dog tags we'd retrieved from the dead commandos onto the surface of his desk. Showing him those had saved Charlie and I a lot of the time we might otherwise have wasted convincing him that our wild-sounding story was true, and the RAF was already beginning to search the waters around Loch Dreich for some sign of the U-boat. Unsuccessfully, so far – it seemed to have dived as soon as the crew had recovered any survivors from the dinghy I'd sunk. Conway glanced up from behind a typewriter and gave us a cheery wave, which I returned, before resuming his perusal of a thick wad of official-looking paper. 'We found the evidence in his cottage.'

'You found some evidence,' I said, sinking gratefully into one of the chairs he'd indicated, and placing the Lee Enfield across my knees, 'which the real traitor planted after murdering him, and staging it to look like suicide.'

Charlie nodded, and remained standing. 'Karl realised after we'd left that he could never have triggered the shotgun from the position we found him in.'

'Not easily,' Protheroe conceded, 'but it's just about possible. What makes you so sure he didn't do it?'

'I know guns,' I said, 'and I know trajectories. The killer picked it up from its usual place by the door, and shot him with it from there.'

Protheroe thought about it. 'Possibly. But the codebook...'

'Check it again,' I said. 'All the ciphers have been used, haven't they?'

'They have.' Conway picked it up from the desktop and leafed through it. 'How did you know?'

'Because it would be useless to an enemy agent. They'd have moved on to the next in the sequence. We'll find that one with the radio.' I returned my attention to Protheroe. 'Which I assume you didn't find in Lennox's cottage?'

Protheroe shook his head. 'No, we didn't.'

'Because the spy still needed it,' Charlie said. 'To contact the raiding party.'

'What I don't get,' Conway said, 'is why they'd even bother. If they have an agent here, what would be the point of attacking us directly?'

'It would completely disrupt all the upcoming operations in occupied Europe,' I said. 'Cutting off support from the resistance movements for months to come. The fight back would be fatally weakened.'

'And it would allow the traitor to move up the hierarchy of the SOE,' Charlie added. She gave Protheroe a significant glance. 'Dead man's shoes, and all that.' It was obvious which dead man she had in mind. 'Giving them access to even more sensitive intelligence.'

'So who is it?' Conroy leaned forward eagerly. 'This is better than a Sexton Blake.'

'Someone the Nazis had a chance to recruit,' I said. 'In Norway.'

'Venables?' Conroy sounded incredulous. 'You must be joking.'

'Do you hear anyone laughing?' I asked. 'I'm only guessing at this bit, but I think the BUF badge we found on Lennox belonged to our mystery man. He either got taken prisoner or surrendered on purpose, and used it to prove he was a fascist sympathiser. Then offered to work for them to undermine the Allied war effort, and hasten their victory. Didn't you?'

'Me?' Conroy's jaw dropped. 'How could it be me?' He tapped the plaster cast on his leg. 'I can't even get around without crutches!'

'Which was really convenient, wasn't it?' Charlie said. 'Turning up with your leg in plaster guaranteed you'd be assigned to administrative duties. You processed Jennings' paperwork, didn't you?'

'You really think I broke my own leg just to get into the office?' Conroy laughed, with what sounded like genuine amusement.

'Of course you didn't,' I said. 'But you're a professional actor. The cast's a stage prop, from one of your old theatrical suppliers in London. You can slip in and out of it as easily as changing your socks.'

'That's a bit of a stretch,' Protheroe said, manifestly sceptical, and Conroy nodded in grateful relief.

'Of course it is. I've never heard anything so ridiculous in my life.'

'Except that I've seen you standing on that leg,' I said, keeping my voice light and conversational. 'Just for a moment. Remember when McMahon was in your way in the hut, and you tried to get past him? You took your weight off the crutch and stood on it, because you had to shuffle through the narrow gap he'd left.' This was a complete lie, but I was certain that everything else I'd deduced was on the money, and he knew it too. If he didn't remember the incident in detail, he might just believe he'd betrayed himself.

'We can settle this easily enough,' Protheroe said, trying to be helpful. 'Get the MO to arrange an X-ray. That should prove the leg's broken.'

Conroy licked his lips, a little uneasily. 'Good idea,' he said. 'Let's put this nonsense to bed as quickly as possible.'

'Fine by me,' I agreed. 'Then you can tell us why you murdered Lennox.'

'Not that it isn't obvious,' Charlie said.

'Not to me,' Protheroe said, sounding genuinely bewildered. 'If Con—I mean, if your hypothetical traitor knew an attack was imminent, why bother?'

'Because he knew McMahon was monitoring the frequency he was using,' I said. 'And the U-boat was about to make contact. He needed a diversion. And once the traitor had apparently been unmasked, there was no need to keep listening out.'

'And Lennox made the perfect fall guy,' I added. 'Everyone knew his old boss had fascist sympathies. Once the evidence was planted in his house, no one would look any further.'

'Except we worked it out,' Charlie finished.

'This is ridiculous,' Conway said, his face grey. He grabbed the crutches leaning against his desk, and levered himself to his feet. 'Let's get over to the medical hut and sort out that X-ray.' He glared at me. 'Then we can get back to fighting the Nazis, instead of each other.'

'Wouldn't that be nice?' Charlie agreed. 'After you.' She gestured towards the door with the barrel of her Thompson.

'Ladies first?' Conroy suggested, with an invitational wave.

Charlie snorted. 'Just this once we'll let chivalry slide. I want to keep you where I can see you.'

'And shoot you,' I added. 'If necessary.'

'Charming.' Conroy hobbled towards the door, tucked the right hand crutch under his arm, and fumbled with the handle.

'Allow me.' Protheroe rose to help. Before Charlie or I could object, he was standing between Conroy and us, reaching out for the door knob. 'It can stick a little sometimes...'

With a click, the door swung open and Conroy pivoted through it, lashing out with the crutch, taking Protheroe in the side of the head. The major reeled back, stunned, and stumbled into Charlie, who staggered, cursing like a sailor on shore leave. By the time the three of us had made it through the door and into the entrance hall, Conroy was already vanishing through the front door.

'Seems you were right,' Protheroe said, kicking aside the discarded plaster cast, which had a neat seam up the side.

'Of course we were!' Charlie levelled the Thompson, realised she no longer had a target and pelted in pursuit, hurdling one of the crutches abandoned in the middle of the hall.

We made it outside together and looked around. Dawn was beginning to break, the sky the clear grey refulgence which presages the first blush of sunrise, and a few early risers were beginning to appear.

Then the roar of a powerful engine announced the approach of a despatch rider, who pulled up outside the house and throttled back. Conroy, who'd been heading for the perimeter like a startled rabbit, turned and sprinted back towards him.

'Morning,' the rider said. 'Urgent messages for Major—'

Conroy punched him in the face before he could finish, and dragged him from the machine. Charlie levelled the Thompson again, and snarled with frustration.

'Damn it! I can't get a clear shot!' A burst from the submachine gun would have taken the stricken motorcyclist down along with the fleeing traitor.

'I can,' I said, the Lee Enfield already in my hands. I raised it as Conroy gunned the engine and roared off.

The target was moving fast, more rapidly than anything I'd yet hit, and jinking wildly from side to side in anticipation of what I was about to do. But there was no time to worry about that. Breathe, heartbeat, let the pattern form. Squeezing the trigger without conscious thought.

Conway lost control and skidded out, bouncing a couple of times on the roadway, while the bike slithered to a halt in a shower of sparks. Charlie and I ran towards him, Protheroe panting a few paces behind, and a small contingent of curious onlookers bobbing in our wake.

Conroy was conscious, and glared at me with

unbridled malevolence, his hands slick with blood as he tried to keep pressure on the wound I'd inflicted.

'You bastard! You shot me!'

'That's my job,' I said. The hit had been a clean one, through the leg he'd been pretending was broken; pure coincidence, but I wasn't about to tell Charlie that. 'I thought you'd appreciate the location, since you've had so much practice limping on it.'

'Go to hell,' he invited.

'You'll get there first,' I said. 'They hang traitors, don't they?'

'Unless we can use them,' Protheroe said, appearing at my shoulder a little out of breath. 'To feed our opposite numbers in the Abwehr disinformation.' He glared at Conroy. 'We'll be having a little conversation about your future once you're patched up. Quite how long it'll be is up to you.'

To my astonishment, Conroy laughed.

'You really think the war's going to go on long enough to bring me to trial? Or do you think his lot are going to come riding to the rescue like they did in the last one? The Reich's victory's inevitable!'

Charlie snorted derisively. 'Napoleon thought much the same thing, as I recall.'

'Maybe it is, and maybe it isn't,' I said. 'But as someone once said, for evil to triumph it only needs good men to do nothing. And believe me, we won't.'

'Or the good women,' Charlie added.

SIXTEEN

Colline Sur Mer, Occupied France, 1944

Words she was continuing to live by. As was I.

I melted into the shadows and waited for a knot of running stormtroopers to pass, heading for the bar, and considered my next step. Retrieving the intelligence I was after had just become ten times more dangerous, with the town a hornets' nest of enemy soldiers. I'd be gambling my life for the possibility of saving people I'd never even met.

So of course I didn't hesitate. After waiting for the echoes of running feet to die away, I made straight for the objective.

BY THE SWORD
By Chris Roberson

April, 1941

I CHOSE AN oak tree on the east side of the road for my perch, figuring that the branches were sturdy enough to hold my weight and spaced high enough to overlook the spot where I'd laid the spikes. If I'd picked the oak on the west side of the road I might have been able to take a second shot, and things would have gone differently, but it was my first mission and I made a few mistakes. The damned tree was just the first of them.

I'd parachuted in the night before under cover of darkness, and had so far eluded any patrols. This far behind enemy lines I didn't expect the same level of troop movements as on the front lines, but I was taking every precaution. From what Nelson had said, countless lives depended on the success of my mission, and untold destruction if I failed.

It was strange being back in Germany after so many years, and the area where I had been ordered to intercept the target wasn't too far from the woods where I'd once gone camping with my father as a young boy, a weekend trip away from Berlin. I'd climbed trees back then, too, but without so much as a slingshot in my pocket, and certainly not my full pack and Lee Enfield slung across my back.

Intelligence said that the truck carrying the target would be passing by sometime before noon, but I was ready and waiting by sunrise. After burying my parachute out in the woods and reaching the coordinates, I'd laid a row of caltrops across the road and concealed them with leaves, before climbing the tree on the east side and getting into position. There was the chance that another vehicle might come by and catch a flat before the target arrived, but the only one that passed by all morning was a horse-drawn dairy wagon heading up the road to the nearest village and its wooden wheels clattered harmlessly over the metal spikes without incident. I figured that luck was with me. I suppose that was another mistake.

I ONLY HAD a few more weeks to go at Glendreich when Major Nelson pulled me out of training and told me he had an urgent mission for me. I never wanted to be a spy in the first place so I didn't argue, only to be told that I'd be parachuting into Germany just like the SOE had planned for me to do all along. Only I wouldn't be there to support resistance groups like the others were training to do: I was there to take out a high value target that intelligence said was vital to the enemy's latest weapons development.

I'd been in London during the Blitz, and had seen firsthand the kind of devastation that the Nazis could manage with their regular bombing runs. But how much worse would it be if they could fire off rockets clear on the other side of the Channel and never even expose their planes to anti-aircraft rounds or barrage balloons?

The Germans had been developing a new type of rocket at the Army Research Center at Peenemünde, but early test firings had all been failures so far. The rockets would launch but would quickly destabilize and veer off target. But intercepted communiques suggested that an engineer named Johannes Mueller working at a munitions factory in Bavaria had reportedly perfected a prototype gyroscopic guidance system that would correct the error, though so far it was strictly theoretical. Mueller had been ordered to travel north and deliver his specifications in person, and if the new component was incorporated into the system and successfully tested, the new Aggregate series rockets would go into full production and could start raining down on London by the end of the year.

My mission was to prevent that from happening, or at least to delay it as long as possible. And that meant stopping Mueller from reaching Peenemünde, one way or another.

* * *

THE SPOT HAD been mapped out by the higher ups at the SOE before I'd been tapped for the mission, but the whole thing was on an incredibly accelerated timetable. They had only intercepted the communications about Mueller and his gyroscope the day before, and if I didn't stop him he'd be in Peenemünde by nightfall and behind a wall of security that we wouldn't be able to get past without an entire fleet at our backs. But we knew the route that he was taking up from Bavaria, and we knew when the truck that was ferrying him was scheduled to set out, so this was our window of opportunity. Intelligence was a little shaky past that point, beyond the fact that Mueller would be travelling with an armed escort, likely two or three SS troopers, along with a driver.

I spent all morning sighting through the telescopic scope of my modified Lee Enfield, watching the southern approach on the road for any sign of the approaching vehicle. Other than the dairy wagon that had rattled by around sunrise, there had not been any other traffic all morning, and I was beginning to worry that the intel might have been flawed or mistaken as noon rolled around. Had Mueller taken another route, or had signals been crossed and he'd been driven up the day before? Had we missed the window altogether?

Then the truck appeared in the distance, rumbling around a slow turn in the road a few miles to the south of my position, and it was time to go to work.

I'd spaced the caltrops every few inches across the entire stretch of the road, so that even if the driver pulled all the way over to one side of the road he would still hit the spikes with at least one of the tires. And anything short of a tank tread—or wooden wagon wheels—would be taken out by the spikes, so all it took was one hit and the truck would be delayed long enough for me to take out the target.

As I tracked the truck's approach through the scope, I considered simply shooting the driver through the front windshield and forcing the truck off the road, but there were simply too many variables to consider. There was no way of controlling where a driverless truck would end up, and no way of ensuring that I would have a clear shot at the passenger if I did. The best option was to stick with the script that Nelson had read to me and play it out as the SOE had planned.

As the truck approached the concealed spikes the driver had steered to the middle of the road, so I liked my odds, but even so I was pleasantly surprised to hear not one but two loud reports as the front wheels of the truck barreled over the caltrops. Tortured rubber flapped and tore as both front tires blew out and the truck trundled to an awkward halt right where I'd planned it would do, directly in the line of sight of the oak tree in which I perched, about a hundred yards away.

I worried momentarily that the caltrops would be discovered right away and the enemy would be put on high alert, knowing that the road had been rigged, but fortunately the truck had barreled forward far enough that the rear wheels were a good twenty or thirty feet from the row of spikes, and when the driver got out to assess the damage he didn't seem to notice the caltrops beneath the leaf cover that I'd scattered. The driver checked the front left tire, and called for some of the troopers riding in the back to get out and help him change the flat before discovering that the right front tire was out as well, and began to swear colorfully because the truck only carried the one spare. Someone would have to continue on foot to the nearest town to pick up another replacement tire and bring it back before they could get the truck up and running again.

The mission briefing had planned for the contingency that only one of the wheels would be taken out, and I would have the time that the flat was taken off and replaced with the spare to locate and eliminate the target passenger. But with the truck immobilized for a much longer time than anticipated I had an even broader window in which to choose my shot. And for the briefest of moments I allowed myself to think this was a break in my favor.

Then the SS troopers clambered down out of the

back of the truck, and instead of the two or three armed guards that intelligence had suggested, there was a full half-dozen troopers with carbines slung over their shoulders. I was well concealed behind the foliage high in the branches of the oak, but the second that I took my shot I'd be announcing my position, and I didn't like my odds of taking out all six of them after eliminating the target. But I had to take my chances.

I could just make out the silhouette of a passenger sitting in the cab of the truck with a valise in his lap, but he was mostly obscured by the door and roof of the vehicle. All I could see through the window was his shoulder and part of one arm, no vital spots. I had to wait for Mueller to step out into view to get a clear shot.

The odds slightly improved when one of the troopers was sent hiking back to a town about ten miles south, where the driver thought he recalled seeing a garage as they drove through. That left only five of them for me to contend with. But still Mueller remained seated inside the cab of the truck, with no clear shot available to me. The best I could hope for at the present vantage would be to wound him, and then open myself up to a barrage of carbine fire from the five remaining troopers. I just had to stay patient and alert, and watch for my moment.

Minutes ticked by painfully slowly, one after

another, until it seemed that I'd been watching Mueller through my Lee Enfield's telescopic sight for ages, but then finally he shifted and started to get out of the truck. My finger hovered over the trigger as I stilled my breathing and watched for the engineer to step out into the open.

But he climbed out of the other side of the truck, on the west side of the road, with the bonnet of the truck obscuring his legs and feet from my view. He'd left his valise in the cab of the truck, and was in the process of blowing his nose on a handkerchief he'd pulled out of his coat pocket.

I lined up my shot, holding my breath, preparing to shoot him right through the eye.

And that was my next mistake. I had a clear shot at any point on his body from the waist up, and could have gone for a center mass shot and gotten a clean kill. Even if the shot didn't kill him immediately he would have bled out before medical attention could be delivered. But it was my first mission in the field, and I was feeling cocky, and so I was going for the headshot. And not just the head, but through his damned eye. Making a bullseye of the poor bastard's face.

But there he was with his watery eyes and his runny nose, and just as I was gently squeezing the trigger to fire the killing round, Mueller was suddenly rocked by a violent sneeze, snapping his head forward. So the bullet that should have driven straight through his right eye and out the back of his skull instead grazed the top of his skull and impacted into the dirt behind him.

I could hear the troopers shouting as they unslung their carbines and scanned the treetops for my position, but my attention was on Mueller, who was reeling from the shock and pain of the bloody—but decidedly nonfatal—injury. I swore under my breath and worked my rifle's bolt to chamber another round. But even as I was lining up to take my second shot, Mueller suddenly collapsed—fainting, I assumed—and I could hear a nasty cracking sound as his head hit the ground.

The bastard had fallen on the ground on the other side of the truck, and now his entire body was shielded behind the truck's bonnet. I could just make out one of his feet sticking out in front of the ruined tires, and the best I could have hoped for from that vantage was to shoot off a couple of the man's toes.

Not that the five troopers on the ground were giving me that chance. Already the shots from their carbines were tearing up the foliage around me, leaves and bits of bark sent flying, and even with their evidently shoddy marksmanship it would only be a matter of time before one of them managed to get a lucky shot in and wing me at best, or put a bullet through my chest or my head at worst, before I could draw a bead on each of them in turn. I might be able to take out two or three of them first, as the original mission briefing had suggested, but not all five. And with the target still alive I couldn't run the risk that the enemy might take me off the board before I had eliminated him, or the whole thing would have been for nothing.

My only chance was to beat a hasty retreat, reassess the situation, and then take another pass at eliminating Mueller before the truck got moving again. Maybe I could lose the troopers in the woods, swing back around to the other side of the road and approach from the undergrowth, keeping low and out of sight.

All of which rushed through my mind in the split second it took me to make the decision, while I slung my rifle onto my back and started to scramble back down the way I'd come up.

Which was when I made my next and most costly mistake, or at least it was when I discovered that I'd made it already and was now paying the price.

I'd been so preoccupied with setting the trap and preparing for the contingencies that I hadn't spent enough time planning my escape route. I'd taken it for granted that I'd be able to take out the armed escort and even the driver once I'd eliminated Mueller, and my worst-case scenario was that one of them would get in a lucky shot and take me out after the mission was complete. I'd also failed to take into account that it would be a lot more precarious getting down out of the towering oak than it had been getting up, especially with shots fired from a handful of Nazi carbines hitting the bark and branches around me every few seconds. And it hadn't been terribly easy making the ascent in the first place with my rifle and pack to weigh me down.

All of which contributed to my foot missing one branch while I misjudged whether another was strong enough to hold my full weight, and as it snapped beneath me I grasped at the open air and fell a good thirty feet straight down to the ground.

I landed on my left leg, hard, and heard a sickening crack. I pitched forward onto the dirt, the breath driven from my lungs and a jarring shock of pain shooting up my leg.

Even through the pounding in my ears I could hear the sound of the troopers approaching from the disabled truck. For the moment I was hidden from their view by the dense stand of trees and the considerable undergrowth, but it wouldn't take them long to find me. I had to get moving if I had any hope of completing my mission.

But when I tried to get back on my feet I found that I couldn't support my weight with my left leg, and even the attempt was enough to send another piercing shard of pain shooting through me. Barely able to stand, I didn't like my chances for walking, but I had to get moving. Holding onto the barrel of my Lee Enfield and setting its stock on the ground, I used the rifle as an improvised crutch and began to hobble deeper into the woods, away from the oak that I'd used for my perch.

Every step brought more pain, and my heartbeat thudded like a deafening barrage in my ears. The sound of the troopers' carbines firing sounded distant and small, but I didn't know whether they had me in sight and were taking careful aim or just firing blindly into the trees and hoping for the best. With the sheer amount of bullets whizzing through the air all around me it didn't seem to make much difference, as the longer I stayed in the general vicinity, the greater my chance of catching one of their bullets and going down for good.

I had my improvised plan of moving north a distance through the trees, then cutting across the road to the west side unseen, in order to loop back around and take another shot at Mueller from concealed cover in the undergrowth. The idea of getting down off my feet and crawling along on my belly was a tempting one, as every time I put any weight on my left foot pain shot through that leg. But I wouldn't be able to move at more than a literal snail's pace that way, and I needed to put more distance between myself and the pursuing troopers before I even stopped to catch my breath. And now the horizon was playing tricks on me, and I could feel myself losing my sense of balance as I took each agonizing step forward.

It seemed as though I'd never reach the edge of the treeline, and a small distant part of my mind worried that I'd lost my way and might actually be circling back in the direction of the enemy. Then the next painful stagger forward brought me out of the trees and into the open air beside the road. I felt a sudden moment of anxiety that I had emerged too close to the truck, that I might be in sight of the driver or any of the troopers that had remained to guard him and Mueller—but a quick glance showed that the road curved gently a short distance to the south of my current position, with the trees obscuring me from the view of the truck and it from me.

Now I had only to make it to the far side of the road and into the sheltering undergrowth before continuing on low to the ground and assessing the situation. A distance of perhaps a dozen yards separated me and the trees lining the west side of the road, a span I could have crossed in a matter of seconds if I was at my best. But with my leg and my increasingly swimming head I was far, far from my best.

If anything, stepping out onto the road was even more painful than trudging through the leafy ground beneath the trees. The pavement was hard and unforgiving beneath my feet, even with me keeping my weight off my injured leg as much as possible. By the time I had taken three steps onto the paved surface,

I could scarcely see straight, the pain was so sharp and all-consuming. The barrel of my rifle dug into the palms of my hands as I leaned heavily on it while swinging my right leg forward, and I had difficulty maintaining my grip on it through sweat-slicked hands as I tried to shift my left leg and reposition the rifle's stock against the pavement. I must have mistimed the motions or misjudged the distances. When I went to shift my weight back onto the makeshift crutch, the end of the stock skittered across the pavement and I pitched forward, completely off balance.

I hit the surface of the road hard, landing on my right shoulder with my other arm outstretched, the rifle clattering to the pavement beside me. Thankfully I avoided hitting my head, but that was about the only thing that I had to be thankful for. I had twisted my legs in the fall, and my left leg screamed in agony as I tried to get my hands beneath me and push back into an upright position. And then I heard a sound approaching from the south, and getting louder.

My first thought was that it was the SS troopers, quick marching in unison, their packs and carbines rattling, but the sounds were all wrong. A rhythmic rattling sound accompanied by a gentle clopping, more like the noise that my rifle had made clattering to the pavement than the noise of footfalls and equipment shaking.

My vision blurred and my thoughts were fuzzy and

dim as the world seemed to close in around me. I reached for the rifle laying on the pavement beside me, figuring I would make a last stand of it here and hold out as long as I could, but my fingers fumbled on the Lee Enfield's stock, and I couldn't seem to get a grip on it.

My last thought as I began to slip into unconsciousness was a brief flash of recognition as I looked up and saw the horse-drawn dairy wagon from that morning coming up the road towards me. And then everything went to black...

I WAS WADING through piles of stinging nettles as high as my knees, looking for my father in the dark. We were camping in the woods, but in the strange logic of dreams we were also in a park not far from our home in Berlin, and all of my classmates who had joined the Hitler Youth were pursuing us through the bushes and trees with loaded carbines, calling out for me in a name that I hadn't used since childhood. I couldn't call out for my father lost somewhere out in the shadows, because they might hear me, and the stinging nettles grew thorns that tore through my clothing and scored my skin and every step was agony...

I woke with a start, my heart pounding in my chest, pulse thudding in my ears. I was in a dark space that smelled of fresh cut hay and earth, my hair matted to my head with sweat, my clothes damp and clinging to my body. My lips were dry and cracked, and my tongue felt oversized and swollen in my mouth. My head ached, my right shoulder felt tender and abused, and my left leg felt like it was encased in concrete. I tried to sit up, but lacked the strength to do much more than shift my arms before I felt myself slipping back down into unconsciousness. I couldn't keep my eyes open, and the darkness closed in all around me once more.

THERE WERE BRIEF moments when the world swam into view and I was lucid enough to take in my surroundings in a little more detail, but for most of the following day and night I struggled through feverish dreams, pursued by hostile forces in dark and thorny woods as I tried to accomplish a vital mission, the details of which I couldn't seem to keep straight in my head. When I woke, the floor beneath me was wooden and strewn with straw, and the air was musty and dry. I had the impression of a roof somewhere far overhead, rather than open sky, so I knew that I couldn't still be out in the woods alongside the road. There was an obvious solution to the mystery that I wasn't quite grasping: I was coherent enough to realize that, but the answer seemed always just out of reach. And then inevitably the darkness would reclaim me and the dreams dragged me back down.

I REGAINED CONSCIOUSNESS with my eyes still closed, but I could see light through the lids, broken intermittently by shadows, as I felt a cool dampness press against my forehead. Wary and more lucid than I'd been for quite a while, I eased my eyelids open slightly to survey the situation.

'Ah, you are awake,' said the woman who knelt beside me in German, holding a damp cloth. 'Ready to rejoin the living?'

She was wearing an apron over a woolen skirt, her light blonde hair tied up in braids, with a scattering of freckles across her nose and cheeks but the hints of crow's feet wrinkles at the corners of her eyes and lines beginning to show on her forehead. Her arms were muscular and her hands callused, but her touch was gentle. I estimated her to be somewhere between thirty and forty, aging well but showing her years. And judging by her accent, a German national.

Had I been captured and not realized it in my hazy confusion? My eyes darted around, looking for any sign of my rifle or sidearm or knife.

My sudden suspicions must have been evident, as the woman smiled slightly and reached out to pat my shoulder before saying, 'No need to worry, you are safe with us. The SS do not know that you are here.'

I struggled to sit up, only managing to lift myself onto my elbows with the woman's help. Looking down I could see that wooden slats had been strapped on either side of my left knee, keeping the leg immobilized.

'My father and I set the broken leg,' the woman explained, following my gaze, 'but we had nothing to treat the pain. The cries of agony in your delirium frightened our horse, so that we had to keep him in the pasture overnight. When your fever finally broke at sunrise this morning, though, I knew that you would recover soon.'

'The wagon...' I began to say in German, but found my mouth too dry and lips too parched to properly form the words, and managed only an inarticulate croaking noise.

The woman reached beside her and picked up a glass, lifting it to my lips. The water inside was cool and soothing, and I guzzled it greedily until it was empty.

'Yes,' she said as I drank, 'I was returning from making our morning delivery to the village when I saw you laying in the road. I had passed a truck where a man was tending to an injured comrade and heard soldiers calling out in the woods, so I knew that they must have been searching for you.'

That explained the smell of hay. I was in a barn.

But why had a woman who evidently worked on a German dairy farm taken in an enemy combatant and hidden him from her own people? And where were my things, my weapons and equipment?

And what had become of Mueller? Was my mission a complete failure, after all?

'How...?' I grunted as I pushed myself all the way up into a sitting position, my hands resting against the wooden floor. 'How long...?'

The woman held up two fingers.

'Two nights have passed since I brought you here, and it is now near midday.'

That long? If Mueller had survived his injuries he would already be in Peenemünde by now, and I had utterly failed at my mission. Assuming that he hadn't died out there on the road.

'The injured man you saw,' I said, measuring my words carefully, not sure whether she knew the role that I'd played in putting him there, 'did he survive?'

'Too soon to say,' the woman answered, 'but the talk in the village is that it is a near thing. They say the poor man has not yet regained consciousness at the inn where the village doctor is treating him.'

My pulse quickened. 'So he's still alive? But still *here*?'

'The farm is half an hour from the village by wagon, perhaps an hour or so by foot. Sooner if you hurry. But I don't think you'll be going anywhere too soon or in too much of a hurry on that.' She nodded in the direction of my splinted leg. 'The break was clean and should set well, but you won't be up and moving for some time yet, I would say.'

Then she gathered up the damp cloth and the empty water glass, and climbed to her feet, sparing a sympathetic glance in my direction.

'I'll bring you something to eat shortly,' she said as she made her way to a door set into the far wall of the barn. 'In the meantime try to conserve your strength, and let your body heal.'

She pulled the door slightly ajar, slipped through quickly, and then pulled it shut behind her.

So my mission was not yet a failure, and I still had a chance to prevent Mueller from delivering the component that would make the enemy's new rockets operational. But I would need to move quickly, avoid any more stupid mistakes, and hope very much that luck was with me.

WITH A BIT of difficulty and more tries than I like to admit I got my feet back under me, though I had to lean heavily against a post while I tried to get a handle on favoring my right leg to keep as much weight as possible off my splinted left. I found my boots in the far corner of the barn along with my pack, but there was no sign of any of my weapons. I could feel hunger gnawing my insides, and knew that there were some field rations in my pack, but I could conserve them if the farm woman was willing to feed me while I hid out in her barn. With my impaired mobility there was no telling how long it would take me to make it back to the extraction point, assuming that I survived carrying out the remainder of my mission, and I needed those rations to last me as long as possible.

Brushing bits of hay off my stockinged feet I managed to get my boots back on, though it wasn't easy lacing them both up when I couldn't bend my left leg at the knee. The splints extended past the soles of my feet, so even with the boots in place the wooden slats held the majority of my weight when I leaned on my left foot, transferring most of the impact to my thigh where the upper set of straps were tied in place, keeping the force off my foot and the broken shin. I could stand and walk with a manageable level of pain, though it remained to be seen how quickly or well.

I tried my hand at moving around the barn, testing out the limits of my mobility. With a little trial and error I worked out a kind of shuffling gait that allowed me to drag my splinted left leg forward with every step and then shift my weight to take a step forward with my right. It was a somewhat noisy and ungainly bit of locomotion, but it beat trying to hobble along with a makeshift crutch.

Assuming that the village where the unconscious Mueller was being treated was as close as the farm woman had said, and assuming that I could keep up that awkward gait more or less continuously the whole distance, I figured that I could reach it in perhaps an hour, two at the outside, assuming that I was able to move unobstructed and wasn't having to keep to concealed areas to avoid being detected. If there were any enemy troops in the vicinity, I would have to exercise quite a bit more care and the going would be considerably slower. And it was a safe assumption that enemy troops would still be in the area, quite likely still on the lookout for the sniper that had eluded them in the woods. Namely, me.

Before I could set out for the village, I needed to get my weapons back. And I needed to get a better sense of the surrounding terrain.

With my shuffle-step gait, I crossed the floor of the barn to the door in the far wall that the woman had exited only a short while before.

Daylight spilled through the cracks around the edges of the door frame, and I quickly determined that the door wasn't locked or latched from the other side. Turning the wooden handle I eased it open fractionally, enough to peer through the gap.

I could just make out the back of a humble but solidly-built farmhouse to my left, about fifty or sixty yards from the door of the barn. To the right stretched a fence behind which I could see a handful of dairy cows grazing, and beyond that the pasture where the draught horse whose lodgings I'd usurped was contentedly munching on a bale of hale.

I heard footsteps coming from somewhere out of sight to my left, from the direction of the farmhouse, but I couldn't see who it was or what direction they were going. I took a chance and eased the barn's door open just a little wider so I could get a better view, while taking pains to keep out of sight myself as much as possible in case any hostiles were nearby.

The footsteps I'd heard belonged to a boy about six or seven years of age, idly wandering down a gravel path that led from the rear of the farmhouse and around the side. It appeared that there was little danger of the boy noticing me, as he was walking aimlessly in the general direction of the dirt road with his full attention on something he was reading, though whether it was a book or pulp magazine or something else entirely I couldn't tell from my vantage point.

I opened the door a little wider and leaned my head out tentatively, taking in more of the surroundings. I could see that the gravel path led past the farmhouse to a hardpacked dirt road that stretched out through the woods. Presumably it connected with the main road where the dairy wagon had come upon me, and from there to the village to the south. That would be the route that I'd follow to reach Mueller.

I was still regaining my strength and conscious of the pangs of hunger from my gut, and my head was still a little light, because I allowed myself to get distracted studying the terrain and calculating the odds of getting back to the village undetected and didn't notice that the little boy had turned around and looked up from his reading material, and was now staring directly in my direction. There was a wide-eyed expression on his face that I couldn't quite read, perhaps curiosity or wonder but just as easily fear or apprehension, like he was rooted to the spot and couldn't take his eyes off me.

My first instinct was to bolt back to cover in case the kid called out in alarm and unseen enemies came running, but without so much as a sidearm or knife, much less my Lee Enfield, it wasn't as if I had great odds at making a successful stand of it if they did. I kept put, and instead treated the kid to as friendly a smile as I could muster, along with a quick wave.

The wide-eyed look still frozen on his face, the kid raised one hand and returned the wave, seeming more than a little uncertain. Had he not known that a foreign agent was hiding out in his family barn? Or had he known full well but was unsure whether I was a threat to him or not? Or was it simply a child's uncertainty when encountering a stranger?

It would have to remain a mystery for the time being, because before I could do much more than blink an old man came around the side of the farmhouse carrying a pair of empty milk pails by their handles in one hand, the metal sides clanking together with each step. As soon as he came into view the old man saw the little boy standing frozen and staring in my direction, and then turned to see me peering through the partially open barn door.

The old man scowled when he saw me, and I expected trouble, but instead he marched over to where the little boy was standing, put his free hand on the boy's shoulder, and steered him in the direction of the farmhouse without saying a word. He pulled open the back door of the farmhouse and hustled the kid inside, then paused before entering himself to glare back over his shoulder in my direction. I could see him mouthing something beneath his breath, but couldn't make out what it was he was saying. Then he slammed the door shut behind him.

My stomach growled, and I could feel my leg muscles straining after maintaining the unfamiliar and awkward gait. I could do with a rest and something to eat. I was getting tempted to break out the canned rations in my pack when I heard the back door of the farmhouse open again. My first instinct was that it was the old man coming back out to make trouble for me, but when I looked in that direction I saw the woman who had tended to me earlier hustling from the farmhouse with a cloth-covered plate in one hand and a mug in the other.

Leaving the door slightly ajar I retreated back to the center of the barn, and settled myself into a sitting position atop a bale of hay with my splinted leg sticking out straight in front of me. I didn't see any point in trying to conceal from the woman that I'd been up and moving around, which would have been immediately obvious as soon as she saw my booted feet, but I didn't see any point in alerting her to the fact that I was planning my exit soon.

Nudging the door open wider with her hip before stepping inside, the woman smiled as she carried the plate and mug over to me. She handed me the plate first before pulling off the napkin that covered it with a little flourish, the gesture a little grander than the pair of bratwurst and crust of bread that were revealed. The mug that she handed me was filled with cool, clear water.

'Thank you,' I said quickly before taking a sip, still feeling the thirst.

'Hilda,' she said, tapping herself on her breastbone. 'Please.'

'Thank you, Hilda,' I repeated with a slight smile.

She started to turn to head back out when I caught her eye and nodded in the direction of the house.

'The boy,' I said, 'is he your son?'

A wistful expression flitted across her face, and she nodded slowly.

'Gerhard turned six years old this past winter.

His...' She paused for a moment, and then continued, 'He is a blessing to me.'

I had a sense I knew what she had been about to say, but not what the significance of it might be.

'And the boy's father?'

Her eyes narrowed, and her expression darkened. For a moment I thought I might have given offense; it looked as though she might turn on her heel and walk out without another word. But then she drew in a deep breath, composed herself, and looked me squarely in the eye as she answered plainly.

'My husband has been in a labor camp since Gerhard was a baby,' she said matter-of-factly, and let the statement hang in the air while she watched for my reaction.

I had heard stories about the Nazis rounding up 'undesirables' since shortly after my father had moved our family to the States. And darker rumors about what became of those who were sent off to the camps. But why had Hilda's husband been taken while she and the boy's grandfather had been left behind on the farm?

'Is your husband Jewish?' I ventured. 'Or some sort of political dissident?'

Hilda's jaw tightened and her eyes narrowed even tighter before she answered.

'No, our family is not Jewish nor is my husband particularly political,' she said, and then without another word she hustled out of the door and closed it behind her, leaving me alone in the barn.

As MEAGER AS the fare was, the food that Hilda had brought was enough to sate my appetite for the moment, but when I was done I felt drained and logy. My left leg was feeling the effects of my exertions, and even with the splints to keep my full weight off my foot and lower leg there was still a considerable amount of pain to manage with each step, though not nearly as much as it would have been had the break been supporting my full weight, as I knew full well from my first stumbling attempts before I'd worked out the trick of it. But all of it combined left me feeling exhausted, and I allowed myself to lay back on the hay and rest my eyes for a moment before moving on to the next step in my improvised plan.

I must have been more exhausted than I realized, because when I opened my eyes again the interior of the barn had been plunged into darkness. Night had fallen.

I didn't like my chances of travelling overland through unfamiliar terrain in the dark, and couldn't run the risk of carrying an electric torch to light my way with search patrols likely still scouring the countryside for me. Even though it meant additional delay, the wisest course of action was to stay put until first light and then set out in the direction of the village. But in the meantime, I needed to retrieve my weapons.

I managed to locate an oil lantern hanging on a hook near the barn door and a box of waterproof matches, and by its light searched the interior of the barn for any sign of my rifle, pistol, or knife. I thought perhaps they might have been stashed away in the rafters overhead, but there didn't seem to be any ladder built into the structure of the barn that I could use to climb up and find out. Thinking that a stepladder might be stowed away or laying on the ground behind the hay I did a thorough search, all the while trying to work out how I could climb with only one leg to rely on. Maybe I could pull up my full weight with both hands while shifting my right leg from each rung to the next, letting my left leg hang down loose and hopefully avoid any painful jarring? But there was no ladder to be found, so it hardly mattered in the end. And from the floor of the barn with the light of the lantern, I couldn't see any spot overhead where the Lee Enfield could be completely hidden and I didn't see the barrel or stock sticking out anywhere, so it was more likely that my weapons were elsewhere on the farm.

Assuming that Hilda hadn't left them laying back in the road where she'd found me, that was... but no, she might have left the rifle laying on the ground where I'd fallen, but it didn't seem likely that she would have taken the time to locate and remove the other weapons I had on me with the SS closing in on her position. It was more likely that I'd been disarmed while I was unconscious, and Hilda or her father or even her son had hidden them from me, perhaps fearful that I might wake up and turn the weapons on them. Was that the dark look that I'd seen in the old man's face as he glared at me over his shoulder? Was there fear in that glance, or just hatred and disgust?

In any case, if I was to regain my arms I needed to search the farm and find them. After the barn, the most likely place where they would have been taken was the farmhouse.

Dousing the light of the lantern, I hung it back on its hook on the wall, and then slowly eased the door open. Outside the sun had long set and the stars shone overhead, but by moonlight I could see the surroundings, though gray and indistinct. I could make out the shadowy mounds of cows sleeping in the pasture beyond the wooden fence, but there was no one moving about outside. The gravel crunched beneath my feet as I shuffle-stepped across the path in the direction of the farmhouse, where I could see faint outlines of golden light spilling around the edges of the curtained windows.

Moving as quietly and stealthily as my awkward gait would allow, I approached the rear of the farmhouse. My intention was to peer through the edges of the window, determine whether Hilda and her family were still up and about, and if so continue to search the outside of the house for any place where my weapons might have been hidden. If Hilda and the others were asleep then I might chance getting inside and searching for them in the interior. But I had taken only a few steps, making no more noise than a few faint footfalls, when the rear door of the farmhouse swung open wide and light spilled out into the night.

Blinking against the sudden glare, I saw Hilda framed by the bright golden light, holding a basket in both arms. As my eyes adjusted, I could see that she was momentarily confused to find me standing out in the open, but then the confusion melted as a broad smile crossed her face.

'I was bringing you dinner,' she said, nodding in the direction of the basket she carried, 'but as long as you are here you might as well come in. Get inside where it's warm and eat along with us.'

She took a step outside and moved to one side, gesturing for me to come up the steps and into the house.

It was not how I'd intended to get inside the farmhouse to search for my weapons, but it got me through the door, and while we ate I figured I could look for the most likely hiding spots in the interior and search them as soon as I had the chance. I didn't much care for the idea of having to overpower or threaten the family, but the success of my mission was vital, and I had to weigh the alternatives. The lives of countless civilians in London hung in the balance, and the feelings of a family of dairy farmers in Germany hardly seemed enough to outweigh all of that. I had no intention of bringing harm to German civilians, but if a stern word or threatening glance regained me the use of the rifle I needed to carry out my mission, it would be a sacrifice I might have to make.

THE OLD MAN and the little boy were already sitting at the dinner table when I followed Hilda into the farmhouse, hands folded and eyes closed as they bowed their heads.

'We have a guest joining us tonight,' Hilda announced, then waved me towards an empty chair across the table from the little boy. 'You can sit across from Gerhard.'

The old man kept his hands folded together and head bowed, eyes squeezing shut even tighter, but the little boy opened his with a look of surprise and his gaze followed me as I shuffled across the farmhouse floor and pulled out the empty chair to sit down.

I managed to shift myself into a sitting position on the chair with some difficulty, my splinted left leg sticking out awkwardly to one side, and rested my hands on the edge of the table with my right leg in front of me.

The little boy kept watching me with his eyes wide the whole time, and a strained silence seemed to stretch out between us, as if he was expecting me to do or say something before he knew how to react, and I wasn't entirely sure what it was.

'My name is Karl,' I finally said, looking for a way out of the silence.

'And I am glad that you are here, Karl,' Hilda said as she set a bowl, fork, and spoon down on the table in front of me. 'It has been too long since we last had a guest to dinner.'

The old man finally opened his eyes and set his hands down on either side of his plate, glaring in my direction for a brief moment before glancing up at the ceiling.

'Scripture tells us to love our enemies and to pray for those who persecute us,' he said, his tone strained, 'but it also tells us that all those who take the sword will die by the sword.'

Hilda was carrying a stew pot in from the kitchen, and nudged the old man's shoulder with her hip as she passed by.

'If your enemy is hungry, give him bread to eat. If he is thirsty, give him water to drink.' She set the pot down on the center of the table. 'Isn't that what you always taught me?'

The old man laced the fingers of both hands together, and glanced at me from under his brows.

'All of my life I have strived to be peaceable with all men,' he said by way of answer, but didn't sound too happy about it. I could see that my presence was a point of contention between the two, but I couldn't quite parse what the opposing views on the matter might be.

Hilda took her place on the chair opposite the old man, and briefly folded her hands and bowed her head with eyes closed before taking up a ladle and doling out servings of the stew into each of our bowls in turn. I could see vegetables, potatoes, and lentils in it as she handed me my bowl, a little thin and without any meat in evidence, but it smelled good and my stomach growled greedily. I picked up my spoon and prepared to dig in when I caught sight of the little boy staring at me across the table again, as if waiting for me to do something, but I still wasn't sure what it was.

As I ate, my eyes scanned the room, looking for any likely places where my weapons might be stashed. Taking up the sword might mean I would die by the sword, if the old man was to be believed, but if so that was a choice that I'd already made, and willingly.

I couldn't help but remember Madame Defarge and her family, on the road to Dunkirk. Another farm, another family of civilians caught in the conflict, taking in a wounded combatant. But this time I was the one with the broken bones needing the help of kindly strangers, and the family Defarge had welcomed our help in driving out the hostile foreigners who had invaded their own country, while to Hilda and her family I was the foreign interloper. From the old man's comments and manner it seemed he objected more to my role as a combatant than to what side of the conflict I was fighting for.

Everyone ate in silence and I was well on my way to polishing off the bowl of stew when the little boy finally piped up.

'You don't talk like an outlander,' he said in a quiet voice. 'You talk like a German.'

I swallowed a mouthful of stew and then nodded slowly.

'I was born in Germany, and I lived in Berlin until I was fifteen years old.'

He stared at me for a moment, chewing that over.

'But you are a soldier for England?'

'Gerhard,' the old man chided, 'such things are not fit topics of discussion...'

'The boy is curious about the world,' Hilda cut in, ladling another helping of stew into her bowl, 'so let our guest speak.'

All eyes turned to me.

'We left when all of my classmates began joining the Hitler Youth, and my father didn't like the idea that I would be forced to join them. We moved back to the United States where my father is from, and I finished school there. And now I'm here to help the English, and to try to keep innocent people from being hurt.'

The boy cast his eyes down with a pained expression on his face.

'I do not want to join the Hitler Youth, either,' he said in a voice scarcely louder than a whisper. 'The other children at school...'

The old man reached over and took one of the boy's hands in his own, comfortingly.

'Take heart, Gerhard. Our family follows the dictates of our faith, not the whims of those who would persecute us.'

The little boy still seemed uneasy.

'But isn't that what you said about my father...?' he began, then trailed off when Hilda set her spoon down on the table with a loud clattering sound, a hard expression on her face.

'I think that is enough curiosity for now,' Hilda said, dabbing at the corners of her mouth with a napkin and then standing to begin collecting the empty bowls. When she'd gathered them all up, she stood at my elbow and smiled down at me. 'I'm sorry that we cannot offer you a place to sleep in the house, but the barn should be warm and dry tonight.'

It was clear that I was being invited to leave, and so, leaning heavily on the edge of the table, I pushed myself up onto my right foot before swinging my left leg around and gingerly getting myself into a standing position. It was just as clear that these people were not my enemies, and had no more love for their current leaders than I did, and as much as I needed the return of my weapons I didn't have the stomach for threatening them with violence to get them. Not yet, anyway, and not unless absolutely necessary. These were peaceful people who had taken in a stranger in distress, and I wasn't about to reward their kindness with betrayal.

'Thanks for the meal,' I said, nodding in Hilda's direction as I made for the door, taking one last chance to look for any likely places where they might have hidden away my weapons, in case the opportunity arose that I might just grab them and leave. But I didn't see any likely hiding places.

Hilda followed me to the door, and when we reached it she pulled it open for me to step outside. As I passed her, she reached out a hand and touched my arm.

'They took my husband because he would not fight, and because he brought word to others about our faith,' she said softly but with conviction. 'I only wish to keep my son safe, and away from any trouble. I do not support this war, and I do not wish harm on anyone.'

She studied my face as she spoke, watching my reaction.

'I understand,' I told her. She had taken me in to keep me from suffering at the hands of the SS, and not so that I could go on to bring harm to her countrymen, combatants or not.

She nodded slowly, then closed the door behind me, and when it was shut I could hear the sound of a key turning in the lock. I wouldn't be getting back inside that way that night, whether they were asleep or not.

With my shuffling step, I made my way across the gravel path and back to the barn. It was not as cozy as the farmhouse, but as Hilda had said it was warm and dry, and a better place to pass the night than out in the elements. It seemed unlikely Hilda would be eager to return my weapons if I simply asked, so I would have to wait and find them at first light and be on my way.

I DIDN'T KNOW all that much about farming, and probably even less about farm animals, but even I knew that dairy cows were milked in the morning. Before the war a farm that size would likely have any number of farm hands working to help run things, but it seemed like it was just the family to keep things operating now, and that meant that Hilda and her father would be busy milking the cows first thing in the morning. With them out of the house that would be my best bet to find where they had stashed my things and start making my way to the village.

I slept lightly that night amidst the hay bales, waking

up at every sound of trees rustling in the wind or animals calling out in the dark, but rested well enough that by the first light of dawn I was ready to be up and moving. I hadn't done much more than remove my boots before I laid down to rest the night before, and it was marginally easier getting them back on and laced up with the splint after the trial and error of the previous day. I secured my pack and left it laying on the floor of the barn just inside the door, where I could retrieve it quickly and be on my way as soon as I recovered my rifle.

Then I slipped out of the door and into the dim morning. The sun was still below the treeline to the east, but the eastern sky was already starting to brighten while the skies to the west were still cloaked in night. Looking to my right I could see that Hilda and her father were seated at stools beside two of the cows, already busy filling milking pails.

The little boy Gerhard was sitting on the back steps of the house reading again. He was staring at some kind of pamphlet or tract, his fingertip trailing along each line of text as he silently mouthed the words, concentrating intently.

I could see that the rear door of the farmhouse was slightly ajar, so I only needed to get past the boy in order to get inside, and from the look of things Hilda and her father would be busy with their milking long enough for me to thoroughly search the interior for my things. With any luck I could retrieve my gear, get my pack from the barn, and be shuffling up the road towards Mueller and the completion of my mission by the time the sun had fully risen. Even if Mueller had begun to make a recovery since the last update Hilda had gotten on the village gossip, chances are he wouldn't have set out for Peenemünde so early in the day, and worst-case scenario I would see his transport passing on the road as I made my way south and I could improvise. I still had some caltrops in my pack, or barring that I could take out the driver and force the vehicle off the road, and then make sure that Mueller had been eliminated. It would be messy and quite a bit more chaotic than the SOE's original mission called for, but it would get the job done.

But first I had to get past the little boy on the steps.

He must have heard the sound of my footfalls on the gravel path, as Gerhard looked up from his reading with an expression of startled panic on his face as I approached. His panic subsided when he saw that it was me, but only marginally. Almost as an afterthought he suddenly put the pamphlet he'd been reading behind his back and out of sight, and tried to act like this was a perfectly natural posture for him to be in.

With my splinted leg and the necessity to keep my weight off the front of my left foot as much as possible I had needed to lean heavily to one side to swing my left leg up and put my weight on the splint by my heel before taking a step up with my right when I'd entered the farmhouse the night before, and I'd needed the full width of each of the wooden steps to pull it off. I needed to get Gerhard to move out of the way before I could attempt it, and with him awkwardly hiding whatever it was behind his back he didn't seem in any hurry to move.

Maybe I could reassure him that I didn't care what he had been reading, put his mind at ease that he had anything to fear from me, and then he could be on his way and I could be on mine.

'Must be pretty good,' I said, nodding in his direction. 'Same one you were reading yesterday? I was always partial to Westerns when I was a kid, cowboys and the Old West and all of that. My father always thought that I should pay more attention to the classics, read the kinds of stuff that would teach me things, make me more worldly, but give me a story about a guy with a six gun and repeating rifle on a horse and I was happy. I sometimes tried to hide what I was reading from him just to keep from getting the lectures, so I understand.'

I gestured in the direction of whatever it was that the little boy had behind his back.

'I won't judge you for what you read,' I went on. 'I promise.'

He looked up at me with a wary expression on his face, but kept his hand behind him and out of view.

'My mother doesn't like me to…' he started, before a voice shouting from my right interrupted him.

'Stay away from him!'

I turned and saw that the old man was heading my way from the pasture, carrying a full milk pail in one hand and pointing an angry finger at me with the other.

'You have no business with the boy,' he said as he drew nearer, 'and he has none with you.'

The little boy kept his eyes on the ground, and now clutched whatever it was that he'd been reading to his chest, protectively.

'I was just asking him about what he was…' was as far as I got before the old man cut me off with a wave of his gnarled hand.

'I have no quarrel with you, but I have no interest in anything you have to say. Now, I let my daughter bring you here to mend, but now that you are up and about why don't you just be on your way and leave us in peace? We want nothing to do with your war.'

I'd told the others back at training that I wasn't cut out for the cloak-and-dagger business, and if this didn't prove it then I didn't know what would. Couldn't talk my way past a little kid or bluff my way past a frail old man. I decided it was time to try a simpler tactic and take the direct approach.

'I'll leave right this minute,' I told him, squaring my shoulders, 'but not without my rifle. Hand it over and I'll be on my way.'

The old man glanced in the direction of the farmhouse, and I could see that he was considering it.

'I don't like having an instrument of death in my home...' he said in a quiet voice. At least now I knew that the Lee Enfield was hidden somewhere in the farmhouse and not abandoned out in the woods, which was one step closer to getting it back and getting on with my mission. 'But I would not have my hands stained by association if I returned it to your keeping and you carried on with bloodshed and killing.'

I wasn't in the mood to argue the justified use of force in the defense of a civilian population with a pacifist, and I doubted very much that I'd sway his opinion even if I tried. Besides, his own son-in-law was already a prisoner of the Nazis because of his refusal to fight, among other crimes apparently, so it wasn't as if the old man hadn't already considered the consequences of inaction.

'Look, old man, just tell me where you've stashed my weapons and I'll go, and you can wash your hands of it all you like. I'm not here to trouble you or any of your family.' I left unstated, for the moment, the possible threat of violence against him if the old man refused to hand them over, but from the look on his face it seemed that the thought had already occurred to him.

He was opening his mouth and preparing to answer when he was interrupted by the arrival of his daughter carrying a pail of milk in either hand.

'Oh, good, you are up and moving,' she said, treating me to a smile. 'I am glad to see that...'

She trailed off as she glanced in the direction of her son and her eyes widened with a look of surprise that quickly blended into one of suspicion as she narrowed her gaze and glared at Gerhard. She unceremoniously deposited the pails on the ground on either side of her, so quickly that milk slopped over the edges, and then reached over to snatch the pamphlet out of her son's hands.

'Where did you get this?' she said, looking from her son to the pamphlet and back again with a hard expression on her face. 'Who gave you...?'

Her jaw set, she turned towards the old man, waving the pamphlet in his face. Closer up I had a better look at it, and could see that it was published by something called the Watch Tower Society. I'd seen similar pamphlets and publications back in the States, handed out by people going door to door evangelizing. Jehovah's Witnesses. They'd always seemed harmless enough, but apparently the Nazis had different ideas on the subject.

'This is what got my husband thrown in a labor camp, Father. Do you want the same fate to befall your grandson? You know that I keep the faith, but we have to be careful!'

So that was what Hilda had meant about her husband

being taken away for spreading the word about their faith. He must have been caught distributing religious materials that the Nazis had outlawed. That explained a lot.

'We are called to act,' the old man said simply, standing his ground with a defiant look on his face.

'There are more of these?' Hilda went on. 'Where have you hidden them?'

The old man scowled for a moment, then set his milk pail down on the ground beside the others and trudged up the steps past Gerhard and into the house. He returned a moment later carrying a shallow cardboard box. He held them out to his daughter, and I could see that there were dozens more copies of the pamphlet stacked inside.

'I am not ashamed of my beliefs, and I did not raise you to be, either.'

Hilda threw her hands in the air in exasperation before reaching over and yanking the cardboard box out of the old man's hands.

'It is not shame, it is caution. It is fear! Don't you understand what they would do to Gerhard if they caught him with these?' She turned to me, cheeks flushed red with anger. 'They remove children from the homes of those who defy the bans against our faith. Any who are caught attending meetings, or distributing literature, or even just in possession of things like these... They send them to other schools far away, or orphanages, or to the private homes of strangers where they can be brought up as 'good Germans,' never to see their own families again.'

She shook the box angrily to punctuate her words, and a few of the pamphlets fell to the ground like falling leaves. Gerhard climbed down from the steps, bent over, and picked one of them up with a mournful look on his face. I got the impression that this was a conversation that the family had been through many times before, and it was clearly wearing on the kid.

'Would you dishonor the strength of your husband's convictions?' the old man shot back.

'My husband would want me to keep our child safe!' Hilda shouted. 'I promised him as they dragged him away that I would!'

Tempers were flaring, and it didn't seem that this would be resolving itself anytime soon. But the door was open and Gerhard was no longer sitting on the steps, so there was nothing barring me from just going into the house and searching for my rifle. The old man and his daughter were so preoccupied with their discussion that I could probably be up the steps and at the door before they even realized, and I didn't think either of them was up to the task of physically restraining me. So long as they didn't kick my leg where it was broken, that is, and I had to hope that the both of them were too gentle for that.

But I didn't get the chance to see if I could make it,

as the discussion was interrupted by the sound of an engine approaching up the dirt road.

'Oh, no,' Hilda gasped, eyes wide with alarm. She turned to me and shoved the cardboard box into my arms. 'Please, take this and go hide in the barn!'

She saw the few pamphlets that had fluttered to the ground and were still at her feet, and scrambled to snatch them up and shove them back into the box.

'We won't betray your presence, I promise,' Hilda said with urgency, 'but they mustn't find you here!'

The sound of the approaching engine was getting louder. Whoever it was would be rounding the corner and into view at any moment.

I WOULD JUST be able to get to the barn and get the door closed behind me, but it would be tight. Without another word to Hilda or her family, I shuffled across the gravel drive as quickly as I could manage. I didn't have time to take care, and more than once my full weight fell on my left foot and I choked back cries of agony. But the splints held in place, and I managed to remain upright and keep hold of the box of elicit pamphlets. I drove my shoulder against the barn door and fell through just as I heard the sound of car wheels crunching on the gravel drive, and nudged the door shut with my right foot. The pain from my leg was overwhelming, but I didn't have the luxury of laying around waiting for the agony to subside.

My pack was still resting against the wall of the barn beside the door, and I grabbed it by the strap and dragged it across the straw-strewn floor towards the nearest hay bale, with the box tucked up against my chest with my other hand. I shoved the pack and the box behind the bale, then dragged myself over to the wall. Faint light shone through the cracks between the wooden boards that made up the barn's sides, and putting my face right up against the wood I could just manage to peer through the gap.

An open-topped car was pulling to a stop beside the farmhouse, with military markings. There was an SS trooper in battle dress behind the wheel, another in the passenger seat behind him and two more in the back seat. I couldn't be certain from my vantage point, but they looked like they might have been part of the armed escort that had been with Mueller in the truck, that had pursued me in the woods a few days before. My suspicions were confirmed when the driver turned off the engine and called over to Hilda and her father, who were standing near the back steps of the farmhouse trying to look unthreatening and unsuspicious.

'An enemy agent was seen not far from here recently, and evaded capture in the surrounding woods,' the driver said, sounding like he was reading from a script that he'd repeated more than once in recent days. 'Have either of you seen or heard any evidence of enemy forces in the area?'

Hilda and her father exchanged an uneasy glance, feigning innocence, and then shook their heads in unison.

'No,' the old man said, 'nothing of the kind.'

The driver, hands still on the wheel, looked around at the surroundings, taking in the pasture, the cattle, the gravel path and the barn.

'Should we continue on, sir?' asked the trooper in the passenger seat.

The driver sighed. I got the impression that they had been carrying out these sorts of searches of farms and households in the surrounding area ever since I had evaded them in the woods, and it had become routine to them by now.

'No,' the driver answered with a labored sigh, 'get out and search the premises, as usual. We need to be sure.'

The car doors swung open and all four troopers climbed out, pulling carbines from inside and slinging them over their shoulders. From their expressions and postures none of them seemed to have much enthusiasm for the search. I thought that might work in my favor. Maybe they wouldn't be as exhaustive in their hunting if they were just working by rote, and I could remain undetected until they went on their way.

Gerhard was hiding behind his mother's skirts,

watching the troopers with a fearful expression on his face. One of the troopers glanced in his direction and smiled, and Gerhard ducked out of sight behind his mother, his small hands gripping tightly to the fabric of her dress as if he might fall into a deep pit if he ever let go. The trooper chuckled at the sight of it, but didn't seem suspicious as to the reason for the little boy's fear.

The driver nodded in the direction of the farmhouse and pointed to one of the other troopers.

'You're with me, we need to search the house.' Then he turned and gestured first to the pasture and then towards the barn, and glanced in the direction of the other two troopers. 'You two search the barn and the field. The sooner we're through here the sooner we can get back to the village and get something to eat.'

The driver and the trooper with him approached the rear steps of the farmhouse where the family was still standing, and for a moment I wasn't sure whether the old man might try to block their passage. Hilda's father was scowling disapprovingly, but so far had kept any comments or criticism to himself. I could see Hilda casting nervous sidelong glances at her father, and it seemed that she wasn't entirely sure whether the old man would be able to restrain himself in the presence of the soldiers, either.

'We need to search the premises,' the driver said matter-of-factly when he reached the steps, and then waved his hand in a distracted gesture to motion for Hilda and her family to move aside.

'Of course,' Hilda said with only the hint of a nervous quaver to her voice, 'we have nothing to hide.'

She turned and put a hand on her little boy's shoulder to steer him off the steps and onto the gravel path, and motioned for her father to follow. There was a tense moment when the old man remained silent and immobile as a stone statue, staring the driver down, but then Hilda's father relented, averting his eyes and stepping off onto the ground and moving to stand beside his daughter and grandson.

Once the driver was at the top of the steps I couldn't see him anymore from my vantage point through the gap in the barn wall, but I could hear the sound of the farmhouse door opening and shutting, so presumed that he and the other trooper would be occupied searching the interior. I could only hope that they weren't thorough enough in their searches to find wherever the old man had hidden my weapons inside, because if they did they would be on high alert and wouldn't stop their search until they'd found me.

Meanwhile, I had the other two troopers to worry about.

If they had followed the driver's orders to the letter and gone straight to the barn to begin searching, that likely would have meant real trouble for me. My first instinct was to drag myself behind the bales of hay and hope that they made only the most cursory of inspections from the door, because if they fully entered the barn and made a more thorough search they were certain to find me.

So when the two troopers waited until their superior was out of sight before pausing to light up a couple of cigarettes and lean on the fence rail, I had a moment to consider my options. In my earlier explorations of the barn I'd been on the lookout for any kind of farming implements or hand tools that I might make use of—shovels, hoes, even axes—but even though there were rusted hooks mounted in the back wall that had obviously been used to store exactly those kinds of tools in the past, they had all been removed. Presumably Hilda—or more likely her father—had taken out of the barn anything that I might use as a weapon while I had been unconscious, perhaps unsure whether I would use one against them when I woke up. All that I had at hand were some bales of hay, a box of religious literature, and a pack with my rations.

Unarmed, with limited mobility and with nothing on hand that I could use as a weapon of any kind, I didn't have any hope of overpowering two armed enemies at once. Even if I could manage to take one of them down and get his weapon, the other trooper would've had ample opportunity to take a shot in the meantime. My only hope was to take them on one at a time and catch them unawares.

If I could incapacitate one of the troopers and take his sidearm, or better yet his rifle, then I would have much better odds of taking out the others. Of course, doing so while the driver and the other trooper were still in the farmhouse would risk catching Hilda and her family in the crossfire. I knew that I would take pains not to take any shots that might put the family at risk, but I couldn't count on the SS troopers being quite so careful.

The most favorable options I had were either to stay out of sight and undetected until the search party moved on, or barring that, to hope that I could catch one of the troopers on his own and take him down before the others knew that I was there. All other alternatives meant extremely long odds for me and serious risk for Hilda and her family.

When the two troopers by the fence finished their cigarettes and stubbed out the butts under their heels, I was tensed and ready to move. If they headed towards the barn next, I could get behind cover and hope that they were as sloppy in their search as their manner suggested. If they went for the pasture instead, then I had a few more moments to consider my odds. But when the two opted to split up to save time, one of them heading off to search the pasture and the other making for the barn, I felt like things were finally starting to break in my favor.

I had a split second to decide whether to try to keep out of sight and hidden or to take advantage of my unexpected fortune and take the trooper on. The urgency of my mission to eliminate Mueller still weighed on me, and every minute that I wasn't heading into the village to take him out was a minute closer to him recovering and making his way to Peenemünde. I had waited long enough.

Rather than hurrying over to crouch behind the bales of hay, I moved to the side of the door, beside the hinges opposite the handle. The door swung open, and so when the trooper entered I would be momentarily hidden behind the door. He would be able to see me well enough once he'd taken just a couple of steps inside, but for a brief instant I would have an advantage over him. I just had to make the most of it.

The boards that made up the wall of the barn were fitted together more snugly beside the door, so I couldn't see outside to track the trooper's progress towards the door. But I could hear his boots crunching over the gravel path, and could tell that he was getting closer. The way I figured it, I had one shot at this. All it would take would be for him to kick me in the left leg or knock me off balance long enough to draw his sidearm or unsling and aim his rifle, and that would be the end of me. So I had to bring him down before he knew I was there. And hopefully without making enough noise to alert his comrades, so I would have enough time to arm myself with my weapons and prepare for my next move.

I remembered the kinds of 'dirty tricks' fighting training that we'd been taught back at Glendreich, the sorts of holds and throws that were most effective at taking down an armed opponent. Of course, if I had my knife I'd simply have punched it into the side of his neck and ripped out his throat before he could cry out. But even without a weapon I still had options. Approaching the enemy from behind, it seemed that the most likely hold would have involved grabbing the little fingers of one of his hands and wrenching his arm back up behind him. But that would give him time to scream out for help, and I wanted to take him down silently if at all possible... which meant that a choke hold would be the better option. So I would have to move in quickly the second that he walked through the door, and try to avoid making any stupid mistakes.

I heard the footsteps from the far side of the wall getting louder, and then the sound of the doorhandle turning and the door began to squeak open on rusty hinges. Light streamed in through the open doorway, and the shadow of the trooper fell across the straw-covered floor of the barn. From the shadow I could see that one of the trooper's hands was on the doorhandle and the other hung loose at his side, so he wasn't currently holding either of his firearms. He didn't expect to find anything in the barn, and wasn't on alert. It was a mistake on his part, and likely the last that he would ever make.

I heard the sound of his boot stepping onto the wooden floor of the barn, only slightly muffled by the thin carpet of straw, then another footfall. One more step and he would be far enough in the barn that he could see me standing behind the door if he just turned and looked back over his shoulder, so I couldn't let him take that next step.

Keeping my weight on my right leg as much as possible, I shouldered into the door, forcing it to close behind the trooper while I stepped forward and wrapped my right arm around his neck from behind. I had already grabbed hold of my right wrist with my left hand and was tightening my hold on him into a vice-like grip before he had even had the chance to raise his arms and try to break free.

The trooper thrashed about, throwing an elbow back that slammed hard into my side, knocking the wind out of me. He kicked behind him with one foot, but missed either of my legs and only succeeded in leaving himself off balance as I tightened my grip around his neck even more. He gasped for air, but I kept the pressure on, choking off his trachea and preventing him from taking another breath. Gradually his struggling ceased, and after what seemed like an impossibly long time he hung limp, and his head lolled to one side.

I eased his lifeless body to the floor of the barn, making as little noise as possible. I didn't think that the sounds of his thrashing around and gasping could have been heard outside the barn, and certainly not as far away as the pasture or the farmhouse, but I didn't want to take any chances.

The dead man had a Luger P08 in a holster on one hip and a bayonet in a scabbard hanging at the other. I considered simply tucking the pistol into my belt, but then thought that the bayonet might come in handy. I had a moment to spare, so instead I unbuckled the dead man's belt and fastened the whole thing around my waist. Then I turned my attention to his rifle, which had fallen to the floor beside him.

It was a Karabiner 98K Mauser, like the one I'd taken off a dead sniper during the retreat to Dunkirk the year before, and like that one, this one had also been fitted with a scope. Maybe my luck had turned, after all. With a scoped rifle of that quality, I didn't need to retrieve my Lee Enfield from the farmhouse to complete my mission. If I could get out of the back of the barn and into the woods undetected, shielded from view of the house and searching troopers, I could be on my way to the village.

I was shouldering back into my pack and looking

for the most likely boards in the back wall of the barn to dislodge when I heard voices from outside raised in alarm.

Had the dead trooper's absence been noticed already? It had only been a matter of minutes since he entered the barn, and if he had been doing a thorough search he wouldn't even be finished yet. So what was the cause of the commotion?

And then I heard Hilda's voice, her distress evident even at a distance and muffled through the wooden walls of the barn.

'No, leave him alone! He's just a child!'

Casting one last glance at the rear wall of the barn, I made my way back to the spot on the front wall where I could peer through the gap between the slats. Slinging the carbine over my shoulder I leaned forward, pressed my face as close to the wall as I could manage and looked through.

Hilda and her father were still standing near the rear of the house where they had been a moment before, but Gerhard had been dragged up the back steps of the house by the driver, who had evidently just come back out of the house, as his companion was still standing in the open doorway. The driver had taken hold of Gerhard by one arm and was practically pulling the little boy up off the ground.

'I said,' the driver barked, clearly annoyed, 'what are you hiding in that pocket, boy?'

With his free hand, the driver reached down and snatched something out of Gerhard's back pocket. Hilda was wide-eyed, holding her hand over her mouth, while at her side her father seemed to be muttering prayers beneath this breath.

The driver straightened up, and even from my vantage I could make out the printing on the Watch Tower pamphlet that he had taken out of Gerhard's pocket. The little boy must have still had the one that he had picked up off the ground when the troopers arrived, and may have tried hiding it in one of his pockets. But the driver must have spotted it when he came back outside.

The driver evidently didn't need to read much of the text to know what the pamphlet was, because as soon as he saw the front he glanced briefly at the boy and then turned to his mother, with his eyes narrowed and a hungry expression on his face. He'd come on a routine search for an enemy agent he clearly didn't expect to find, and instead had found something else entirely.

'You know the consequences for the possession and distribution of restricted religious materials?' the driver asked, waving the pamphlet back and forth like a miniature banner.

'He must have... found that... somewhere in the woods,' Hilda answered haltingly. 'Or possibly the village. When we went to make a delivery, or...'

It was obvious that the driver wasn't convinced, or didn't care to hear any possible excuses and explanations. He motioned for the trooper still standing in the doorway to step forward, and then shoved Gerhard in his direction.

'Detain the boy,' he said, drawing the Luger from the holster at his hip. 'Where there is one piece of restricted material there may be more. And even if the household isn't involved in the distribution of trash like this, their inability to keep it out of the hands of their child means that he should be removed and taken to a more suitable environment, to be instilled with proper German values.'

He took a few steps away from the house onto the gravel path, looking around until he caught sight of the trooper who was still scouting around the pasture, who didn't seem like he was in any hurry to find anything.

'Finish up out there and come back in,' the driver called over. 'We need to make a thorough search of the house and...'

He paused for a moment, craning his neck and looking around.

'Wait, where is Heinrich?'

The trooper in the pasture looked a little sheepish as he gestured in the direction of the barn.

'We split up,' he called back. 'He's still searching the barn.'

The driver turned and looked in my direction, scowling. Then he cupped one hand around the corner of his mouth like a trumpet and called out, 'Heinrich, finish up in there and come help search the house.'

After a moment's indecision, I stepped closer to the door and called back, 'Yes, sir,' in gruff tones. I didn't know what the dead man's voice had sounded like and hoped that at a distance and muffled by the walls it would be convincing, and as the driver turned around and walked back into the house it seemed like it had done the trick.

I could see that the trooper who had been in the pasture was climbing over the wooden fence on his way back to the farmhouse, with the other trooper still standing on the back steps of the house with Gerhard firmly in his grip. Hilda and her father were standing to one side. The old man was still quietly praying, but his daughter had a look of anguish on her face as she pleaded with the trooper to release her son. From what I could see, the trooper was acting like he couldn't hear a word she said, and she might as well have been talking to a brick wall.

I glanced back over my shoulder to the rear of the barn. My instinct was to dislodge one of the slats and slip out while the troopers were preoccupied searching the house for forbidden religious tracts, and make my way through the woods to the road and before one of them finally found my weapons and discovered that there had been more to find on the farm than a kid with some mimeographed pages. I had some miles to cover before I reached the village where my target was hopefully still convalescing, and the sooner I was shuffling on my way the better.

But if I left with things as they were, I knew that there would be no way that Hilda would be able to keep her family together. The troopers would haul away her son and she would never see the boy again. Gerhard would be shuttled off to an orphanage or some stranger's home, all for the crime of holding beliefs that the current regime had deemed unacceptable. And if the troopers were to locate the cardboard box of pamphlets in the barn, or another like it hidden somewhere in the house, or my weapons and pack, then Hilda and her father would be arrested and taken to a labor camp like the boy's father had been.

I felt searing guilt as I considered leaving them to their fates, after Hilda had risked everything to help out a foreign stranger who she'd found in the road. My mission had to take top priority, and I couldn't risk it all to linger on the farm a moment longer than I had to. I couldn't justify staying behind to intervene, even if it meant...

Then I glanced in the direction of the armored car that the troopers had arrived in. If I remained behind and took care of them, keeping Hilda and her family out of the authorities' grasp for a while longer at least, then I could commandeer their vehicle and reach the village in a fraction of the time it would take me on splinted leg and foot. Of course, it wouldn't be easy to drive with one leg unable to bend at the knee, but I could make do.

So now I just had the three remaining troopers to contend with.

The one who climbed the wooden fence was now about halfway back from the pasture to the house along the gravel path, while the other was still keeping hold of Gerhard on the back steps, with the driver inside the house and continuing his search. I could easily have taken out one of them with a clean shot, and probably have dropped the other before he had time to react, but that would leave the driver still inside and out of sight. So even with the two outside eliminated, the one inside would have time to consider his options, possibly trying to use Hilda or her father as human shields before coming out, or staying out of view and threatening to fire on Hilda and her family to draw me out. Or maybe he'd just start firing blindly through the windows or doorway, spraying and praying, and then I'd run the risk that Hilda or Gerhard or the old man or all three of them would get caught in the crossfire.

I needed to draw all three of them out and into the open before I took my first shot, and then I could take out all three before they had a chance to react.

The most obvious option was the one I liked least, but it stood the best chance of working. My makeshift impersonation of the dead man calling from the barn had fooled them once, so it would just have to fool them again. Or at least long enough for me to draw a bead on all three of them.

'Everyone!' I called out through the closed door in the same gruff tones I'd used before. 'Come quick! I've found something in the barn!'

The trooper on the gravel path stopped and looked in the direction of the barn, an eyebrow raised.

'What was that?' called the trooper from the back steps of the house.

'Heinrich says he found something,' the one on the gravel path replied, and then started moving in the direction of the barn.

The trooper at the back of the farmhouse climbed down the steps to the ground, pushing Gerhard ahead of him, and then propelled the little boy in the direction of his mother, instructing them to keep together and keep quiet. Then he unslung his rifle from his shoulder and turned to call back through the open back door of the farmhouse.

'Dieter! Heinrich has found something in the barn and Friedrich is going to check it out.'

I couldn't make out what the driver answered in reply, but from the trooper's manner it seemed like he was waiting for Dieter to exit before making a move. He took up a position at the base of the steps and aimed his carbine in the general vicinity of Hilda, her father, and her son.

'Keep still and keep quiet,' he barked at the family, as the three of them huddled close together, Hilda hugging Gerhard to her side and the old man continuing his silent prayers.

The trooper on the gravel path—Friedrich, presumably—had his rifle aimed at the ground as he continued towards the barn.

'Heinrich?' he called out. 'What did you find?'

I didn't think that my rough impression would stand up under much scrutiny, and the last thing I needed was for them to see through my ruse and start firing indiscriminately into the barn. So rather than trying to answer again I kept quiet and hoped that my silence would buy me enough time to draw all three of them out into the open.

But my lack of a response was giving Friedrich second thoughts, if the look of growing suspicion on his face was any indication. He was about forty feet away from the door of the barn by this point, his grip on his rifle's forearm tightening as his trigger finger hovered by the trigger guard. I couldn't tell whether he worried that his comrade might be injured and unable to answer—which, in a sense, he was—or that someone might be with him in the barn and preventing him from responding, but it didn't seem that he yet suspected that it hadn't been Heinrich who had called out before. Or if he did suspect, he wasn't sharing his suspicions with the others.

It would only be another moment or two before Friedrich closed the distance and reached the door of the barn. My gaze kept darting from him to the back door of the farmhouse, but so far the driver had yet to emerge into view. The trooper by the back steps still had his rifle trained on Hilda's family, and from the barn door I had a clear shot at both of them.

Friedrich called out again as he approached the barn, concern for his comrade evident in his tone. I kept quiet, maintaining my grip on my purloined Mauser, ready to kick the door open and start firing the second that all three enemies were in view.

The stress of having a rifle pointed at him, on top of everything else he'd been through since the troopers had arrived, seemed to have pushed Gerhard to breaking point, as the little boy had begun to sob, his shoulders shaking and tears starting to stream down his cheeks. His mother held onto him tightly, but remained silent, her wary gaze on the trooper near the back steps.

Friedrich was getting closer. Just a few more paces and he'd be near enough to reach out and pull open the barn door, and I would be exposed. I'd have to take him out fast, because at such short range he'd have to be a pretty poor marksman to miss.

I kept looking through the gap towards the back

door of the farmhouse for any sign of the one they'd called Dieter. The second that he stepped into view I could open fire, but not a moment sooner or I'd risk putting Hilda's family in the line of fire.

'Heinrich?' Friedrich called as he drew even closer. With his right hand wrapped tight around his rifle's grip, finger hovering near the trigger guard, he reached out his left hand towards the handle of the barn door. 'I'm coming in.'

I had to make a move, couldn't wait any longer, would have to make the best of a bad hand when...

The driver appeared in the open back door of the farmhouse, an annoyed expression on his face, with his rifle slung on his shoulder and his sidearm in its holster.

'Heinrich, answer me—'

I could hear the handle of the barn door turning, and immediately went into motion.

Shifting my weight onto the splints on my left leg and gritting my teeth against the pain, I kicked out with my right foot, sending the barn door swinging open and smashing into the face of the trooper on the other side, knocking him momentarily off balance. Then I came down on my right foot, raised the stock of the Mauser to my shoulder, emptied my lungs, took aim at the trooper who was pointing his rifle at Hilda's family, and squeezed the trigger. My shot went in one side of the trooper's skull and out the other, and I was chambering another round before his body even started to fall.

Friedrich had kept his feet and held onto his rifle when the barn door had slammed into him, but it was pointed at the ground, and he had a confused expression on his face, like he was still trying to work out what was happening. Scarcely even needing to aim at such short range I swung the barrel of my 98K around and shot him square in the face.

At the back door of the farmhouse the driver was recovering from the shock of the attack well enough, in the act of drawing his Luger, but it was too little, too late. I chambered another round, took aim, and shot him in the head before his sidearm had cleared its holster.

By the time the body of the first trooper hit the ground, all three of them had been eliminated.

I REMAINED IN the barn for a few moments longer, waiting to make sure that there weren't any other enemy forces coming running at the sound of shots being fired. There had only been the four troopers in the armored car, but there was always the chance that others had accompanied them but peeled off earlier to search the surrounding woods. But there was no sign of reinforcements, no enemies calling out to their fallen comrades. All was silent, broken only by the quiet sobs of a little boy and the startled gasps of his mother.

I didn't know what reaction I'd get from the family for saving them from a squad of SS troopers, but I wasn't prepared for the outrage I faced when I finally shuffle-stepped my way out of the barn and into the open.

'What did you do?' the old man cried out, staring with wide-eyed horror at the body that lay sprawled across the back steps of the farmhouse, then turned to the one laying on the ground a little closer to him with a rifle close at hand. 'What did you *do?!*'

I still had the stock of the 98K to my shoulder, eyes on the dirt road around the corner of the farmhouse, ready to open fire on any enemy forces that stepped into view.

'Kept your grandson out of an orphanage, at the very least,' I answered through gritted teeth, 'and probably kept you and your daughter out of a labor camp, too.'

I swept the barrel of the carabiner around to look in the direction of the pasture, in case any enemy forces had been searching somewhere past the farm and might be approaching from behind, but there was nothing to be seen but cows contentedly chewing their cuds and the draft horse who had evidently been spooked by the sounds of the rifle shots and had retreated to the far end of his enclosure.

'You're welcome, by the way,' I added, glancing

over at the old man.

But it was clear that he was in no mood to thank me.

'You expect gratitude?! After you have murdered these men in our name? Their blood is on our hands now!'

It didn't look as though reinforcements were incoming, so I slung the 98K over my shoulder and shuffle-stepped my way across the gravel path to where the body of the driver had fallen. I didn't know if the model of armored car that they had arrived in required an ignition key to start, but if there was one then it would be somewhere on his person. It was awkward crouching down with my left leg unable to bend at the knee, but I bent as low as I could and dug around in the dead man's pockets and in the pouches on his belt, but turned up only a half-empty pack of cigarettes and a silver plated lighter. I had to hope that the key was still in the vehicle, or this diversion wouldn't turn out to be the time saver that I had hoped for.

Using the Mauser as a makeshift crutch, I pushed myself back up onto my feet to find Hilda had walked over to stand behind me. Her father was still working himself up into a lather about the violence he'd just witnessed, and her son was standing stock still with his eyes on the ground, but Hilda looked like she had moved past shock and grief and whatever other emotions might have surged through her in the last ten minutes or so, and was in the process of gathering herself to do what needed to be done next.

'Other soldiers will come looking for them,' she said simply, pointing to the body that I'd just been searching, then gesturing to the others scattered across the yard.

'More than likely,' I answered. 'They were probably on a routine patrol, not targeting your farm in particular, so chances are that their superiors won't know precisely where they were this morning. And closer to the action they'd probably just be chalked up as missing in action. But yes, this far behind the lines chances are they'll come looking when these boys don't report back in. They'll want to make sure that there aren't enemy forces in the area... well, more than the one they were already searching for, anyway.'

Hilda's eyes were moist with tears that welled up but didn't fall, yet her jaw was set and there was a look of determination on her face.

'You must help us hide the bodies,' she said, like I was a farmhand and she was giving me my orders for the day. 'They can't be here when the others coming searching.'

I couldn't argue with her logic, but I had my own priorities to consider.

'I'm sorry, but I have a mission to carry out. Your

best bet is to drag them out into the woods and bury them, as far from the farm as you can get them.' A brief look of panic flitted across her face as she considered the scale of the task, and I added, 'Or, do you have any neighbors who keep pigs?'

She blinked in confusion for a moment before nodding in response.

'You might ask to borrow one or two of them for a day,' I went on. 'Offer to fatten them up. A couple of hungry pigs can make short work of a body—there's these three, and a fourth out in your barn, by the way—then I'd still recommend burying their gear and weapons out in the woods, as far away from here as you can manage.'

I turned and started to shuffle over to the car where it was parked near the corner of the farmhouse. I paused after a few steps, and glanced back over my shoulder at them.

'You don't want them to find my weapons on your farm either, I'd imagine. I don't suppose you'd return them, after all?'

Hilda turned to look back in her father's direction, but the old man's face closed up tight. Without another word she walked up the steps into the farmhouse, and returned a moment later with my pack under one arm and holding my Lee Enfield with the other.

'Live by the sword,' the old man said as I took my things from her, the scripture sounding more like a curse, 'die by the sword.'

I shook my head.

'I'd love to beat all of them into ploughshares someday,' I said, 'but not today. Yours aren't the only lives at risk, and it's my job to try to keep them safe, for as long as I can. And if I end up dying in the process, then that's my lot.'

'And how much more killing along the way?!' the old man shot back.

'That's my lot, too,' I answered, and made my way to the dead men's car.

I LEANED OVER the driver's side door of the car to look for the ignition switch, and was relieved to see that the key was apparently permanently attached in this model. I reached in and set the butt of the Lee Enfield on the floor boards of the passenger side with the barrel resting against the passenger door, then pulled open the driver's door and began the awkward maneuver working myself onto the seat without jarring my left foot. It took some doing, and in the end I had to twist into a fairly uncomfortable position to get both legs inside and the door closed. The clutch pedal was under my left foot and had to be depressed every time I needed to change gears, which sent spikes of pain shooting up my leg each time I shifted. Just reversing the car out of the farmhouse drive and back onto the dirt road involved no fewer than three gear changes, and my eyes were welling with tears from the pain of holding the clutch down with my broken leg time and again. But once I got the car completely onto the dirt road, I'd just need to shift up through first and second to third gear and I would be on my way.

I was taking a few deep breaths and steeling myself to hold down the clutch to get the car into gear when I caught sight of Gerhard standing by the side of the road. The little boy still seemed shaken by everything that had happened, but his tears had stopped, and he had an unreadable expression on his face.

Hilda was dragging the body of the dead driver across the gravel path towards the barn, no doubt to stow it out of sight with the others until she could work out some way of disposing of them. I hoped her neighbors' pigs had appetites.

Gerhard kept staring in my direction, and I couldn't tell if he was waiting to say something, or waiting to hear something from me, but I didn't know what to say to him. So I didn't say anything at all.

Gritting my teeth against the pain, I pushed down on the clutch with my left foot, shifted into first gear, and then eased on the accelerator. The sun was climbing up the sky in the east, and with any luck I would get to the village before my target was even up and about.

IT WAS EARLY afternoon, and I was on the roof of a garage up the street from the inn. Since I'd been watching, the village doctor had come and gone, and he'd been wearing a look of relief on his face when he came back out. It seemed his patient was on the mend, so chances were that he'd be leaving shortly.

I'd ditched the armored car in the woods just outside the village less than a quarter of an hour after driving away from Hilda's farm. Thankfully there hadn't been any traffic on the road and I had been able to get the car out of sight before anyone saw me, and then made my way into the outskirts of the village without being spotted. Hilda had said that Mueller was convalescing in an inn, and since there was only one in the village I would have been safe in assuming it was the one she meant, even if it hadn't been for the truck and soldiers stationed out front. It was the same truck that I'd disabled with my caltrops a few days before—now with four functioning tires—parked in the lane in front of the inn, with a couple of the SS troopers who had pursued me into the woods standing guard. From their casual postures, it was clear that they didn't suspect that anything untoward had happened to their four comrades who hadn't yet returned from patrol. They seemed almost bored, lounging at their posts with their weapons propped up against the side of the truck, no doubt eager to leave the village behind once and for all.

Through the scope of my Lee Enfield I kept a close watch on the front door of the inn. I'd chosen a vantage point with a clear line of sight, with no obstructions between my position and any of the likely exits from the building. So far everyone had gone in and out the front door, but even if Mueller exercised caution and exited through the rear of the building and out of view he'd have to come out into the open to get into the cab of the truck, and then I'd have him.

I'd also learned my lesson, and taken the time to make sure that I had a quick and direct path to get down off the roof and out of the village once I'd taken the shot, assuming that I wasn't able to take out both of the remaining troopers after eliminating Mueller. If one or the other of them was able to get to cover in time, or weren't out in the open when I had the chance to take the shot at Mueller, I was far enough away that I could get back to the ground and make my way through the village outskirts and into the woods before they could reach my position, even hobbling on my splinted leg, and I would be back in cover before they had the chance to return fire. And I wouldn't be risking another broken leg in the process. I'd made enough mistakes in this mission, and wouldn't make any more if I could help it.

While I kept the rifle trained on the door of the inn, I couldn't help but think about the look on Gerhard's face, or the outraged expression of his grandfather, or the look of quiet resignation and desperation his mother wore as she dragged the bodies of the dead men out of view. Their family had been split apart by the war long before I came along, long before the real fighting had even begun if I understood correctly, but when they'd taken me into their home to recover from my injuries they'd brought the fight right to their own doorstep. I made the choice to keep Hilda's son out of the Nazis' hands for a while longer, at least, but their family would have to deal with the consequences of that decision.

But then I thought about all of the families back in England, the mothers and fathers, sons and daughters, grandparents and more, who had already suffered through months of the Blitz, and stood to suffer even worse if the Nazis gained the ability to attack from across the Channel with impunity. And that the choices I'd made had not really been a question of choice at all, and I had done what had to be done. If the enemy could not be stopped, they could at least be delayed.

Then the front door of the inn swung open, and Mueller stepped into view, looking a little worse for wear with a bandage wrapped around his head and his cheeks a little gaunt and underfed, but otherwise hale and hearty.

For exactly three more seconds.

I emptied my lungs, did a quick bit of calculation for windage and drop, aimed for where Mueller's head would be when he finished taking his next step, and squeezed the trigger.

I held my breath as I chambered another round and swung the barrel around to aim at one of the two troopers who were both scrambling to pick up their rifles from where they were propped against the side of the truck, and dropped the first of them just as Mueller's body began to fall, the back of his head blown clear open. I potted the first of the troopers through the throat as the other was straightening up with his rifle in hand, and caught him with a clean shot through center mass before he had a chance to raise it to aim. Both troopers slumped to the ground as voices began to cry out, the villagers shouting in alarm.

I ducked out of view, and in the confusion managed to make it down the back of the garage and to the ground before anyone realized where the shots had been coming from. One of the villagers saw me hobbling down the lane out of the village and shouted, but I was too far away for anyone to pursue before I reached the treeline and was able to disappear out into the woods.

WITHOUT THE GYROSCOPIC guidance system that Mueller had developed, the development of the new rocket systems at Peenemünde was set back months, even years. Nazi rockets would one day fall on London, but we had delayed that day as much as possible.

My injuries would heal, and there would be other missions to carry out.

I would do what needed to be done.

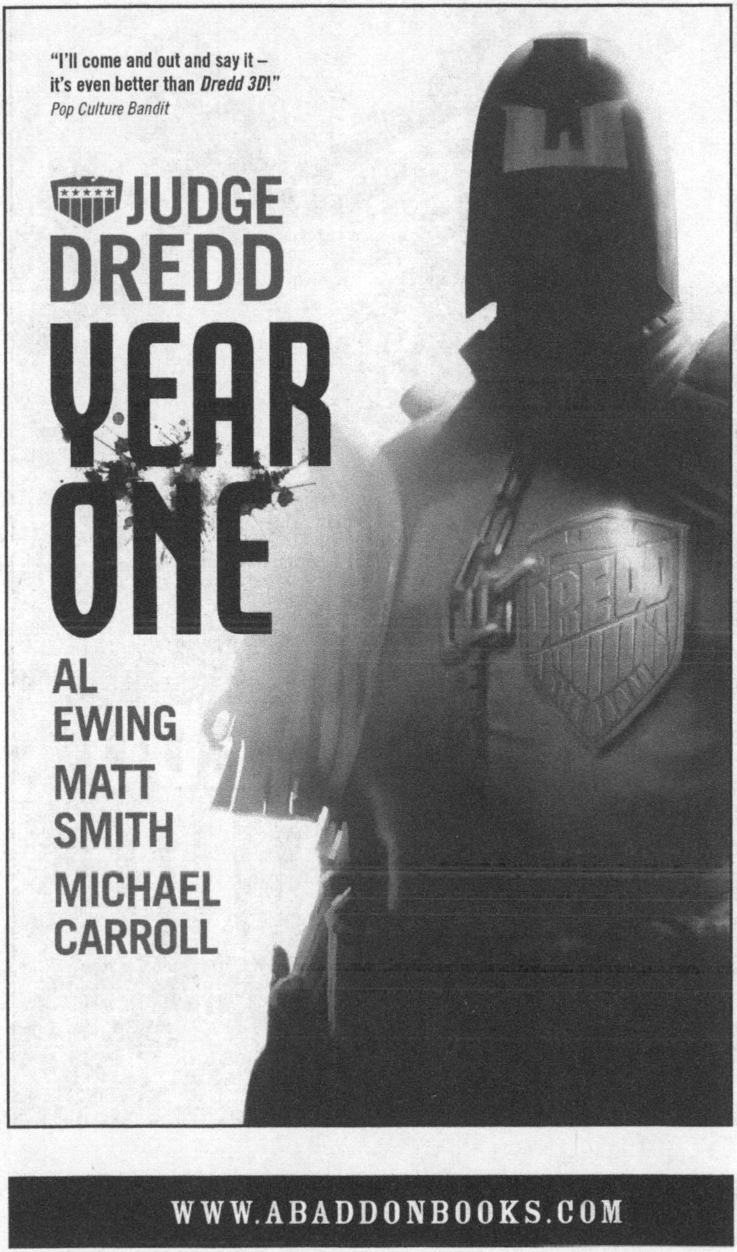
"I'll come and out and say it –
it's even better than *Dredd 3D*!"
Pop Culture Bandit
JUDGE
DREDD
YEAR
ONE
AL
EWING
MATT
SMITH
MICHAEL
CARROLL

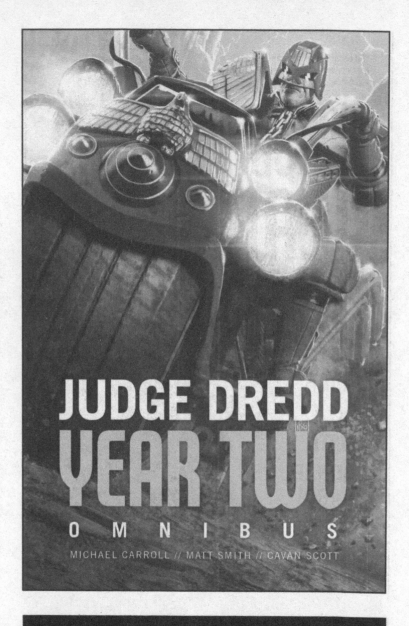

"Takes you inside the head—and out on the beat—of the future's greatest lawman like never before!"

Comic Book News

JUDGE DREDD
YEAR THREE
OMNIBUS

MICHAEL CARROLL // MATT SMITH // LAUREL SILLS

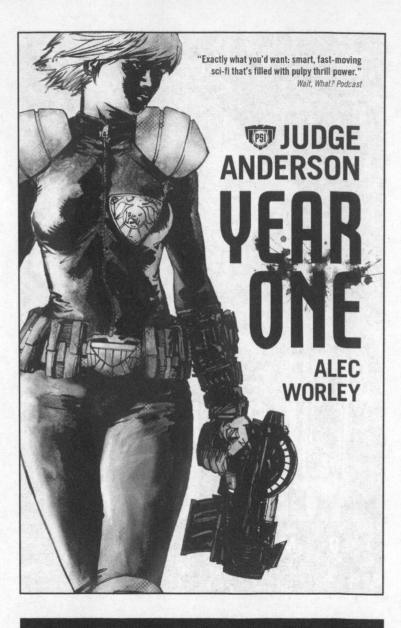

JUDGE FEAR'S
BIG DAY
OUT
AND OTHER STORIES

FEATURING
STORIES BY
ALAN GRANT
CAVAN SCOTT
GORDON RENNIE
SIMON SPURRIER
AND MANY OTHERS

EDITED BY MICHAEL CARROLL

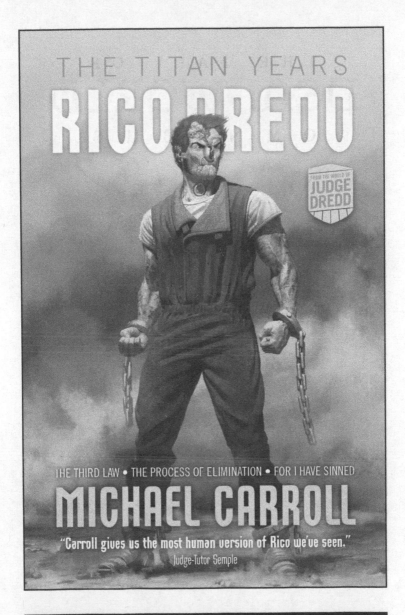

THE FALL OF
DEADWORLD
OMNIBUS

MATTHEW SMITH

FIND US ONLINE!

www.rebellionpublishing.com

/rebellionpub   /rebellionpublishing   /rebellionpublishing

SIGN UP TO OUR NEWSLETTER!

rebellionpublishing.com/newsletter

YOUR REVIEWS MATTER!

Enjoy this book? Got something to say?

Leave a review on Amazon, GoodReads or with your favourite bookseller and let the world know!